"When did you de
rebel wasn't the wa

He studied her face for
contours and planes.

"There just comes a time when you either choose
to grow up or continue down that senseless self-
destructive path to nowhere. It also comes from
finding something you're good at. Something
you're passionate about." He swiveled the chair
and leaned back in it. "For me it was renovating old
houses. I liked the irony of it. I used to break things,
but now I fix them."

A look of dawning washed over her pretty face and
he wanted to kiss her. The same way he had all
those years ago.

"I never thought of it that way, but you're right."

Elle held his gaze and drew her bottom lip between
her two front teeth. He wondered if she was
remembering that kiss and wanting to relive it, like
he was doing.

"Why did you feel the need to break up my
wedding, Daniel?"

Well, there it was. The million-dollar question that he
had both dreaded and wanted to plow into headfirst
just to clear the air. Because until they had talked
about it and it was out of the way, there would be
no moving forward in the direction he was certain
they were destined to go.

**THE SAVANNAH SISTERS: One historic inn, two
meddling matchmakers, three Savannah sisters**

Dear Reader,

To me, family is everything. Mine is a close-knit bunch. It shouldn't come as a surprise when I tell you that I drew on what I know when I wrote *A Down-Home Savannah Christmas*.

The story's heroine, Elle Clark, leaned on her family when she was stood up at the altar. They supported her when she decided to leave Savannah for a fresh start. Now she's home again, and she's come face-to-face with Daniel Quindlin, the best man in her wedding, who she believes convinced her groom to run. She's relying on her family more than ever to shield her from her nemesis. The problem is, they're determined to help her see that Daniel actually *is* the best man...for her.

This is the first book in my three-book Savannah Sisters miniseries. I hope you enjoy it as much as I loved writing it.

Warmly,

Nancy

A Down-Home Savannah Christmas

Nancy Robards Thompson

H HARLEQUIN® SPECIAL EDITION

Recycling programs
for this product may
not exist in your area.

ISBN-13: 978-1-335-57422-0

A Down-Home Savannah Christmas

Copyright © 2019 by Nancy Robards Thompson

Printed in U.S.A.

National bestselling author **Nancy Robards Thompson** holds a degree in journalism. She worked as a newspaper reporter until she realized reporting "just the facts" bored her silly. Now that she has much more content to report to her muse, Nancy loves writing women's fiction and romance full-time. Critics have deemed her work "funny, smart and observant." She resides in Florida with her husband and daughter. You can reach her at Facebook.com/nrobardsthompson.

Books by Nancy Robards Thompson

Harlequin Special Edition

Celebration, TX

The Cowboy's Runaway Bride
A Bride, a Barn, and a Baby
The Cowboy Who Got Away

The Fortunes of Texas: The Lost Fortunes

A Fortunate Arrangement

The Fortunes of Texas: Rulebreakers

Maddie Fortune's Perfect Man

The Fortunes of Texas: The Secret Fortunes

Fortune's Surprise Engagement

Visit the Author Profile page
at Harlequin.com for more titles.

This book is dedicated to Jay Robards
and Russell Prock, adopted Savannah sons.

JJ, thank you for answering my endless stream of
questions and debating whether that smell was
paper mills, pluff mud or something more...impolite.
Thank you for being the very best tour guide.

Chapter One

*B*ridezilla.

Elizabeth Clark's husband-to-be had called her Bridezilla. Right in the middle of their rehearsal dinner.

She'd simply worried aloud to her sisters, Jane and Kate, about the flowers for the ceremony and whether the florist had understood that she wanted the tall arrangements behind the dais, not in front of it where they would block the guests' view of the wedding party. She didn't think Roger was paying attention, since he was seated at the opposite end of the table for twelve.

He must have been, because he called out, "Relax, Bridezilla. Just go with the flow."

There was an edge to his voice, and it carried down the length of the table, past their guests, who had fallen silent in the wake of his words. After Elle had processed the barb, she'd chosen to believe he was trying to be funny.

Sometimes Roger's humor missed the mark and sounded caustic. On the occasions when she reminded him to check his tone, an argument usually ensued. Tonight, on this night when she needed everything to be perfect, she decided to let his quip slide.

She was a good sport. She and Roger were deeply in love.

Even so, she couldn't help saying to no one in particular and everyone in general, "Grooms are lucky. They simply have to show up on their wedding day and everything is done. Poof! Like magic."

She sent Roger an air kiss and a good-natured eye roll.

Everyone, except Roger, followed her lead and laughed.

That was when she thought she'd glimpsed something dark in his eyes.

Over the next twenty-four hours, every niggling doubt and fear that Elizabeth had caged in the way-back of her consciousness had commando-crawled its way to freedom.

Now, as she stood with Roger at the altar in her picture-perfect white dress, in front of their friends and family, holding her flawless bouquet of white and blush peonies, ranunculus and heirloom roses, and listened to the minister proclaim marriage sacred—something that *should not be entered into lightly and only after much consideration*—her doubts and fears waged all-out warfare, like a terrifying premonition that Elle watched come to life in slow motion.

The minister asked, "Do you, Roger, take Elizabeth to be your wife?"

Roger paused for what seemed an eternity. Elizabeth watched the color drain from his face and then he reached up and tugged at his shirt collar, causing his bow tie to cock to the side like an uncanny smirk.

A hiccup of nervous laughter echoed in the crowded church. Elizabeth tried to snare Roger's gaze. If he would just look at her, they would take a deep breath together and everything would be fine. But Roger was staring off into the distance somewhere over her left shoulder, in an anxious trance.

Stay with me, Roger. It's just nerves. Everything will be fine.

He'd never liked being the center of attention. She knew that about her husband-to-be, but for as far back as Elizabeth could remember, she'd dreamed of a humongous wedding. She'd wanted the big white dress, the court of bridesmaids and bushels of flowers.

Most of all, she'd dreamed that this day would be perfect. And it would be. They just had to get through their vows and to the other side of "I do" and everything would be fine.

Elizabeth stole a glance at the 256 people who had gathered at the Independent Presbyterian Church of Savannah to watch the high school sweethearts marry.

Rogabeth. Elloger. They'd been together so long that many already thought of them as one entity.

The minister cleared his throat. "Roger, do you take

Elizabeth to be your lawfully wedded wife? If so, please answer, 'I do.'"

Good God, was he holding his breath now?

If Roger would just look at her, she'd silently remind him to breathe. And not to lock his knees.

Come on, Roger. Don't pass out on me now.

Reverend Chambers put his hand on Roger's arm. "Roger? We need an answer, son."

Roger opened his mouth like he was about to say something, but he snapped it shut again before he could make a sound.

Now Elizabeth was the one holding her breath.

She stole a glance at the congregation. Could a person actually die from self-suffocation…or humiliation?

Breathing was overrated.

Then again, nothing would wreck a wedding faster than the bride dying at the altar. She gulped a breath of air like a drowning swimmer who'd broken the surface.

Now, if Roger would just answer, or nod, or something. *Anything.* Reverend Chambers could pronounce them husband and wife and they'd walk down the aisle arm in arm and out the doors at the front of the church. She'd fix his tie and they'd take pictures. They'd laugh about how he'd almost passed out in the middle of the ceremony and had given her a case of hives.

Come on, Roger.

Elizabeth was entertaining the thought of nudging him with the toe of her shoe. God knew her dress was big enough to hide the prod. But before she could do it, she locked gazes with Daniel Quindlin, best man.

He reached out and gave Roger's shoulder a firm shake.

"Come on, man," he said. "Do the right thing."

For a moment Elizabeth thought Daniel was trying to help. Until Roger found his voice. "I'm…sorry. I can't do this. Daniel's right, Elle. I can't marry you. I'm sorry."

Roger gave Daniel a resolute nod. "Thanks, man."

As the world moved in slow motion, Elle watched her groom exit through a side door. Her sister Jane slid her arm around Elle's waist, propping her up and shielding her from the astonished faces greedily gobbling up the drama.

Elle couldn't feel her legs. Through the blood pulsing in her ears, she heard Jane hiss in a low, venomous voice, "How could you, Daniel? Why couldn't you leave well enough alone?"

Six years later

Elizabeth Clark had been back in Savannah less than twenty-four hours and already she was questioning whether coming home had been the right decision.

Home was the Forsyth Galloway Inn, the sprawling mansion-turned-bed-and-breakfast on Whitaker Street that had been in her family for six generations—more than one hundred fifty years—and had been a thriving business since 1874. She'd grown up in the big Victorian house with its turret, ornate gingerbread and creaking mahogany floors. The place was simultaneously comforting and claustrophobic. It evoked a certain nostalgia, not so dissimilar to memories of Great-Aunt Gertie's overzealous bear hugs. Everyone tried to avoid her hugs, until she'd cornered them and they had no choice but to be smothered in the pillow of her enormous bosom. But years later, when Great-Aunt Gertie and her propensity to invade personal space was gone, her hugs seemed kind of sweet, a throwback to simpler times.

The Forsyth was Elizabeth's smothering hug. When she was there, she couldn't wait to get away from it but it always drew her back when times were tough. Like yesterday, when the bottom had fallen out of her life in Atlanta.

It was the last day of school before the holiday break. Some of the teachers were making plans to go out after work for some holiday cheer, when Principal Wescott had buzzed Elle's room and asked her to come to the office for a quick meeting.

The long and short of it was, her job as an art teacher had been eliminated. She knew her position was tenuous when they hired her two and a half years ago. The money for art education wasn't in the school's budget, but a group of tenacious parents thought art was important. Via the school's foundation, they'd raised enough money to hire an art teacher for two years. The parents thought if they got the art program off the ground, the county would work it into the budget. That didn't happen, and despite raising enough money to cover her salary for the first semester, the foundation finally realized the county wouldn't budge and had redirected its efforts behind a new pet project.

For the foreseeable future, the school didn't have a job for her. Principal Wescott couldn't make any promises, but she said she would try to find Elle another position after the first of the year. There would probably be something in the fall. Not in art, but it would probably be a teaching job.

"In the meantime, I'll understand if you need to look for another job."

Merry Christmas to her.

The timing couldn't have been worse. Elle had applied for a mortgage to buy a condo in the Buckhead area. She'd scrimped and saved and brown-bagged so many ramen-noodle-soup-and-peanut-butter-sandwich lunches that she couldn't stomach the combo any longer. But it had been worth it to get the home of her dreams. She'd saved up enough for a down payment, she'd found the perfect place and the sellers had accepted her offer. Without a job, there was no way she would qualify for the mortgage. It had taken her a long time to find this condo—the perfect size, in the perfect area, at the perfect price. The sellers were building a house. They couldn't hold it for her, and at that price, it wouldn't be on the market long. Her own real estate agent had caught wind of the listing before it went public. They'd moved fast, but without a job, there was nothing she could do. She had to be honest with the lender about her change of employment status.

Mortgage aside, she needed money to cover her expenses while she looked for a new job. She had enough money to cover living expenses for a few months, but after that, she would have to dip into her down payment savings.

At least she had a little bit of leeway. Even so, she hadn't been able to take a full deep breath until she'd packed her car and found herself fifty miles down I-75, heading straight into the big smothering bosom of Savannah and the Forsyth Galloway Inn.

Now, after a fitful night's sleep, she stood on the

wrought iron balcony off her bedroom, sipping coffee from a china cup with a matching saucer and breathing in the heady morning air—that intoxicating punch of the humid subtropical flora, spiced with hints of sulfur from the river. She closed her eyes and inhaled the comforting perfume. No matter how long she stayed away, she could always count on Savannah smelling the same when she returned. She was counting on the sameness of it to help her get her head on straight.

Even in December, Savannah was warm by northern winter standards.

And then there was that sunrise.

It dawned so brilliantly over Forsyth Park, which was decorated for the holidays with pine garlands and red bows wrapped around the old-fashioned light posts and swagged along the black iron fence surrounding the majestic fountain. The vision took Elle's breath away. She was tempted to believe the magical scene was a sign that coming home had been the right move. She stood admiring the splendor of lavender, persimmon and amber blooming in the sky. The fickle breeze flirted with her hair and kissed her cheeks before it flitted away to toy with tangles of Spanish moss dripping from the ancient live oaks in the park across the street.

She sighed and swallowed the last sip of coffee, which had gone cold and bitter.

Yeah, that's more like it.

Cold and bitter. She laughed to herself.

Despite how she wanted to believe this glorious morning with its painterly sky and philandering breeze was a sign of good things to come, she was a realist. Mother Nature wasn't in the business of manufacturing miracles. This was merely proof that life went on—whether or not she had a job that would allow her to take care of herself and not rely on anyone else.

Right now she needed to get dressed for the day and help her mom, Zelda, and her grandmother, Wiladean—or Gigi, as she and her sisters called her—prepare for the breakfast meeting they were hosting at the Forsyth.

She hadn't come home to vacation or freeload. She fully intended to make herself useful.

Last night her family had been giddy when she'd walked in. The corners of Elle's mouth turned up and her heart tugged at the thought. When she'd entered the inn, they'd been in the middle of setting up for this morning's meeting, but they'd stopped what they were doing for hugs and tea. Because what would a home-coming—planned or impromptu—be without a steaming cup of tea?

Of course, there had been questions—

"What are you doing here?"

"I just wanted to see you."

"Is everything okay?"

"Well, I lost my job today, but everything will be fine. I hope."

It was the truth. Somehow, she would land on her feet. She would either find another position as an art teacher or come up with a brilliant career change.

"Is that you, Elizabeth?" a voice called from the sidewalk below her balcony. Longtime neighbor Mercy Johnston was power walking in her black pencil skirt and athletic shoes, no doubt on her way to work at the Chatham County Courthouse.

Elle waved.

"Good to see ya back in town, hon."

"Thanks, Mercy," Elizabeth said to the woman's back as she continued past. "Have a good day."

Keeping her stride, Mercy acknowledged Elle with a flutter of her left hand.

As Elle turned to go inside, she saw the lights flicker on inside the Cuppa Joe, the coffee shop that was located farther down the street. Another longtime neighbor, Lisa Reynolds, did a double take and waved as she opened the doors to the Angel Cakes Bakery, a few doors down from the Forsyth.

A couple of cars whooshed by and the delivery truck for the Chat Noir Café slowed as it lumbered around the corner. The brakes whistled and Elle could picture it parking next to the inn's kitchen door. There was something soothing in all the sameness, the sounds and smells, still knowing her neighbors after all this time and to have them welcome her home without mentioning the Great Wedding Debacle.

In Atlanta, she could be as anonymous as she wanted to be. In Savannah, there was no hiding. Elle felt compelled to hold her chin up and prove that she was *better off* on her own. She could take care of herself; she didn't need a man to take care of her. In fact, it had become a point of pride that she remained free and unencumbered, free do to what she wanted when she wanted, without having to answer to anyone.

Roger had done her a favor by setting her free.

Elizabeth glanced at her watch. The guests would arrive in about an hour. Since she'd kept Gigi and her mom away from their work last night, Elle wanted to get down there and pitch in.

She cast one last wistful glance at the gorgeous, changing morning light glowing in Forsyth Park. Now fingers of silver and gold filtered through the ancient live oaks, painting an ethereal picture. That was when she caught a glimpse of a man jogging past the fountain.

Without her contact lenses, she had to squint to bring the details of his masculine form into semisoft focus. But that didn't matter. He looked *fine,* even from this distance. She leaned against the wrought iron railing and drank in the blurry, virile beauty of him. Taking care of herself may have become a point of pride, but she still appreciated a hot guy.

This hot guy was definitely worth the second glance.

He was tall and lean, with dark hair that might have been a tad too long, and broad, muscled shoulders that looked to be the natural by-product of honest, hard work.

Nice.

Something vaguely familiar emerged through the soft focus.

Wait.

Did she know him? In a town where everyone knew everyone, except for the tourists, it was likely. She did a quick mental inventory of the various places their paths might have crossed. She quickly crossed off her Atlanta circles, people who worked with her at Stapleton Elementary School and the parents of the students in the art classes she taught at the school.

Even though Savannah was home—she was born and raised here—she hadn't spent much time here over the past few years. Not since she'd graduated from Savannah College of Art and Design and moved to Atlanta to teach art after the wedding was called off.

She mentally lined through her list of Savannah neighbors, and the various SCAD-related groups he could've belonged to and found herself reaching all the way back to her days at Savannah Country Day School.

The jogger stopped on the sidewalk across the street from the inn and peered up at her.

Her stomach clenched.

Wait.

Oh, crap.

Is that...? Oh, no, is that Daniel Quindlin?

She turned away too fast. The clumsy motion made her spoon fall off the saucer and clatter on the balcony's wooden floorboards. Feeling foolish, she bent down and retrieved it.

What's wrong with you? He probably saw you do that. Of course he saw you do that.

With a deep breath, she straightened, pulling herself up to her full height and pushing her shoulders back before she stole another glance.

Oh, God. It was him.

Her stomach lurched and she gritted her teeth against a gamut of perplexing emotions. If the pretty sunrise and everything familiar had been an omen of good things to come, Daniel Quindlin was standing there staring up at her like a harbinger of doom.

What was he doing in Savannah? When had he returned? She would've thought her mother or grandmother would've warned her.

Not that it mattered. When they were in high school, he'd made it very clear that Savannah was the last place on earth he wanted to be.

He stared at her for a moment before he lifted a hand in greeting.

Elizabeth's heart thudded and heat burned her cheeks. *Why?* She had no reason to feel embarrassed or care what Daniel Quindlin thought of her. She raked her hand into her hair, trying to casually smooth the humidity-induced bedhead that she hadn't bothered to fuss with before she'd stepped out here with her coffee.

This was Savannah. Not Atlanta. And knowing everyone in town—or at least most of the historical district—was the breaks of being a sixth-generation Savannah native.

She knew better.

Head held high and cheeks still burning, she pulled her hand out of her hair and gave a quick wave to prove that she was fine, that all these years after he'd succeeded in talking Roger out of marrying her and leaving her at the altar, humiliating her in front of God and everyone, she was perfectly fine.

Common sense dictated that Roger couldn't have been talked into doing anything he didn't want to do. But she blamed Daniel for the way it all unfolded. Seeing him again after all these years reopened a wound she thought had healed.

Shortly before the ceremony had started, Jane had gone to her car to get a safety pin. She'd passed by the choir room and had overheard Daniel telling Roger he had no business getting married. She'd heard him say, "It's better to get out now than to get a divorce later."

Jane had beaten herself up for not telling Elizabeth, for letting her walk down that aisle. But Roger had sounded so resolute when he'd told Daniel, "Stay out of my business," and Jane thought Roger was fine. That Daniel was being a jackass.

A few minutes later, when Roger was waiting for Elizabeth at the front of the church and everything seemed to be going as planned, she'd made the snap decision to not say anything to Elle.

Elle had understood. She had forgiven Jane. Actually, she'd never held it against her sister, because it hadn't been her fault. The music had been playing. Roger had been in place, seemingly prepared to get married. What was Jane supposed to do? Stop the wedding over a snippet of conversation she hadn't even been sure she'd heard right?

For a solid year after the wedding Jane had beaten herself up, saying if she had one do-over, she would've confronted Roger and Daniel and asked them to clarify and she would've stopped Elle from walking down the aisle.

For Jane's sake, Elle had tried so hard to prove she was fine that she'd actually convinced herself she was.

Until now.

After all these years, the mere sight of Daniel Quindlin made her feel clumsy and out of control.

But wait—why was she giving him so much power over her? When she thought about it that way, it was easier to push Daniel out of her mind and go inside to get ready for the day.

She wasn't going to get anything done if she stayed out here on the balcony all morning acting like a forlorn Juliet. Instead, she showered and dressed in a lightweight pink-and-green sweater and jeans. She took a couple of extra minutes to dry her hair, smooth it into a high ponytail and apply makeup.

She felt more like herself as she walked down to the kitchen, greeting several guests that she passed on the grand staircase. In the lobby, she paused to admire the stately Christmas tree decorated with beloved family ornaments. It was standing sentry in its usual place of honor, the same spot it had occupied for as far back as Elle could remember.

As usual, her mother and grandmother had transformed the inn into a tasteful Christmas wonderland with wreaths and red flower arrangements, gold beaded garlands, large nutcrackers and boxes wrapped to resemble large presents.

No one was in the kitchen, but a large foil-covered serving pan from the Chat Noir waited on the kitchen's long trestle table. The aroma of breakfast food made Elle's stomach growl. After she washed her coffee cup and saucer and put them away, she lifted a corner of the foil that covered a large aluminum pan. A waft of steam carried the delectable scent of homemade biscuits. She inhaled deeply and replaced the lid. She needed to get out of the kitchen before the temptation to help herself got the best of her.

She pushed through the double doors and into the butler's pantry, which connected the kitchen to the private dining room. Surely there was something in there she could do to help finish setting up for the breakfast meeting?

With its oversize windows and wall of French doors, the inn's dining room was one of her favorite places in the ten-thousand-square-foot house. The room was light and bright and offered a gorgeous view of the inn's garden. This time of year the garden was still green, but the springtime bounty of roses, pink blossomed cherry sage, white pincushion flowers and cheery black-eyed Susans were replaced with voluptuous poinsettias and whimsical Christmas decorations.

While most of the floral paintings that hung on the walls in the dining room were originals Elizabeth had painted while she was in art school, the scene through the French doors looked like a wall-sized holiday-themed painting that changed with the light.

Her wedding reception would have been in that garden. She hadn't even thought about it in all the times that she'd come home over the past six years. All it took was seeing the guy who'd instigated the breakup to make it all come flooding back.

Now he knew she was home, and if he was any kind of gentleman he'd stay in his neighborhood—wherever he was living now—and out of hers. Forsyth Park was a huge green space. All he had to do was stay away from the Whitaker Street side.

A memory flooded to the forefront. It was the day of the wedding, after Jane had helped her escape to the bride's room. Daniel had had the nerve to come to the door. Of course, Jane, her protector, had shifted into full-on attack-dog mode. She hadn't given him a chance to speak, or to explain or gloat or whatever he'd come to do.

Elizabeth had been surrounded by her mother, her grandmother and her younger sister, Kate. They were fussing over her, each one doing her best to console her, while Jane played gatekeeper, answering knocks and taking messages and assuring the well-wishers she would convey their condolences.

Then Daniel had knocked.

Elle hadn't even seen him, but she knew it was him by the how-dare-you tone of her sister's voice. She'd swiftly stepped outside and the rest of the conversation had been muted, leaving Elizabeth to fill in the missing pieces. Her favorite version had Jane chasing Daniel away—literally. Striking a fear in him so raw that he'd turned and hightailed it away.

It hadn't really happened that way, of course, but on the rare occasion that she felt blue over the way things had ended, Elle imagined her sister chasing away the monster.

Elle had even gone so far as to paint a picture of the scene in her art journal, a private book of sketches, doodles and experimental paintings that she showed to no one. The art journal was her catharsis. It was a private place where she could leave what was haunting her on the page and close the book.

She took special care to ensure the painting of Jane, in her pale pink maid-of-honor gown, hadn't looked like a bride chasing a groom in a church.

Because a bride shouldn't have to chase the man with whom she was supposed to spend the rest of her life. What kind of a marriage would that be?

For the first six months or so, Elle had half expected Roger to come back all apologies and remorse, kicking himself for making the worst mistake of his life. She wouldn't have taken him back, of course. But at first she'd imagined him walking through the door, contrite and blaming cold feet on a momentary loss of reason, begging her to give him another chance.

She'd abandoned that foolish daydream in a hurry. She'd traded it in for the belief that she needed no one. She could take care of herself. Never again would she be so foolish.

It hadn't taken her long to get the job at Stapleton teaching first grade. Later, they'd created the art teacher position for her.

She'd moved to Atlanta and moved on with her life. Yeah, and losing that job had sent her back to where it all started. Running into Daniel in the place where everything fell apart wasn't helping.

Well, she wasn't staying long. She'd only come home to regroup, to see her mother, Gigi—and maybe even her youngest sister, Kate, if she could get away from the salon where she cut hair. They were such strong women, and through them she would remember she was strong, too.

She would make it through this temporary roadblock and she'd come out all the stronger for it.

As she watched the red and gold garlands on the garden topiaries sway in the gentle morning breeze, she vowed to herself that she wouldn't dwell on the past. This was a new chapter, a new page for her art journal.

She turned away from the window and surveyed the festively decorated room to see what she could do to help. The tables and the speaker's podium were already set up. Someone had set out holiday themed tablecloths, silverware and china plates and arranged the eclectic mix of porcelain coffee cups, similar to the one she'd drunk from this morning, on silver trays next to the sterling coffee urn. The tables needed to be dressed and set and the food from the Chat Noir needed to be set out.

Where were her mother and Gigi?

Elizabeth lit the Sterno pots to warm the water in the chafing dishes. When she was a kid that had always been her favorite job. Gigi had supervised, but she'd let Elizabeth light the little pots. The thrill she'd felt watching the purple jelly pop into an orange-and-blue flame was a visceral memory and it warmed her from the inside out.

Making herself smile in the spirit of "fake it until you make it," she picked up one of the tablecloths, gently unfolded it and spread it over the closest table. She smoothed the surface a little too hard, trying to get it to lie flat, and she realized Daniel Quindlin was still lurking in the recesses of her mind.

If he was living in her head, it was because she was allowing him to be there. She needed to block him out. She needed to think of something worth dwelling on.

She glanced around the dining room—she had to think of something worthy, like the women in her family who had come before her.

Those women had made the delicate linens—like the one she'd nearly rubbed a hole in as she tried to smooth it out—by hand. Each generation had taken loving care to preserve these heirlooms and pass them down. They were guardians of the legacy. To Elle, the linens and the stories attached to them were nearly as important as the inn itself. The women from whom she and her sisters were descended had taken such pride in sharing their finery—the linen, china, crystal, the silver coffee service and chafing dishes—with the guests who'd stayed at the Forsyth. It was the little touches that made people feel at home and brought them back.

Elizabeth heard the rattle of a food cart in the butler's pantry.

"There you are," her mother, Zelda, said, after she butted open the doors and pulled the food cart through, a smile overtaking her face. "I'm so happy you're home, baby girl, I can hardly stand it."

Her mother's eyes searched Elizabeth's face. Her unasked questions hung in the air.

Last night, Elizabeth had been too tired to get into many of the details. She'd simply said there wasn't money to fund the art department. She didn't want her mother to worry about her. Zelda had been through her own trials and tribulations over the years. As long as the Forsyth Galloway Inn was in the family, Elle would always have a roof over her head and food to eat, but she would never have a lot of extra money. The inn gobbled up most of the proceeds, leaving very little left over. In fact, the place was looking a little tired, like it could use some attention. They still needed to fix the water damage sustained during the last hurricane, and even her beloved dining room would only benefit from a fresh coat of paint. All it took was money.

Elle didn't want Zelda worrying about what she would do for work if the county couldn't place her in another position—or better yet—find a way to fund her job teaching art.

"Thanks for starting the Sterno," Zelda said as she lowered a tray of food into a chafing dish. "On my way down to the dining room, the Gibbons, who are in room twelve, stopped me and said they needed fresh towels. I went to the linen closet to get them some, but it's empty. That's strange because last night when I checked, we had at least three sets of washcloths, bath and hand towels. I wonder where they went?"

Zelda frowned and raked a hand through her auburn curls. She was in her midfifties and still had a shape that most thirtysomethings would envy and a peaches-and-cream complexion that was pretty near flawless except for the worry crease at the bridge of her nose and the faint lines around her eyes.

"I don't know, Mom. I'm sorry. There were plenty of towels in my bathroom. I'd be happy to call the linen service and arrange for a delivery if you want."

Zelda waved her hand. "We had to cut linen service. We do the laundry in-house to save money. It's a lot of extra work, but it's part of the belt-tightening process."

Belt-tightening?

Elizabeth was about to ask if everything was okay when Zelda chatted on.

"You know, to afford this renovation we're wanting to do. But anyway, I was downstairs a few minutes ago throwing in another load of towels. I did several yesterday afternoon, but I didn't have a chance to fold them and put them away. But I know I saw towel sets in the downstairs linen closet last night."

"Someone must've helped themselves," Elle said. "No worries. After we get the breakfast meeting set up, I'll fold the towels for you, deliver a fresh set to the Gibbons' room and restock the linen closet. I'm happy to help out while I'm here."

"Thank you, sweetheart." The crease between her mother's eyes eased a bit. It sounded as if she'd been working hard. Elizabeth wanted nothing more than to lighten her load. While her grandmother seemed to thrive in this business, her mother was more of an introvert.

"Where's Gigi this morning?"

"Lately, she doesn't make it downstairs until mid-morning," Zelda said.

Gigi had been talking about retiring and turning the place over to Zelda. When she did, her mother would need to hire someone at least part-time to help her. Especially on days like this. The Forsyth Galloway was not a one-woman operation.

"You look tired," Elle said as she took a tray of blueberry muffins off the cart and set them on the buffet. "Not in a bad way. You're as beautiful as always. But I worry about you with this load and cutting back staff. Are you holding up okay?"

"Oh, honey, I'm fine. This place is just…" Zelda's words trailed off and her brow furrowed again. "It's fine."

She smiled, but Elle detected a certain note in her voice. She decided to take another tactic.

"Then, if everything here is fine and you're tired, that must mean you're keeping secrets." Elle laughed. "Is there a man who's keeping you up late? Because something's keeping you up."

She wanted to say something to lighten the mood, but she was half-serious.

Zelda snorted good-naturedly and smiled. "Heavens no! Are you kidding? I have no time to meet men. At the end of the day, I go up to my room and fall asleep in front of the television every night because I'm too tired to move."

Zelda had suffered an acrimonious divorce several years ago and hadn't found anyone else. Elle understood why her mom would be gun-shy. The split had been painful. Elle hadn't exactly been gung ho to fall in love again after Roger. So, she understood her mom's hesitation.

"Darn, I was hoping there was a man," Elle joked.

Zelda ignored her. "Doesn't the food smell good? Looks like Moriah outdid herself this morning." Zelda lowered a pan of mini quiche into one of the chafing dishes. Elle did the same with the biscuits and a pan of bacon. Since the inn didn't have a restaurant and only offered a continental breakfast to guests, Moriah West of the Chat Noir Café, a fixture in downtown Savannah, catered most of the events at the Forsyth that required substantial food.

Zelda picked up the tongs and helped herself to a quiche before Elle could cover the dish with a silver lid.

"Taste test," Zelda said before taking a bite. "We need to make sure the food is as good as it looks. In fact, why don't you fix yourself a plate and go in the kitchen and have breakfast? I can handle things in here."

"You are changing the subject, mother." Elle put her hands on her hips and raised her right eyebrow in a challenge. "I hear they have speed dating every Tuesday night at Jack's downtown. Why not give it a try?"

Zelda shook her head and cocked a brow, mirroring her daughter's expression. "I've got too much on my plate with everything that's going on with the inn. But bless your heart, you seem to be interested. Why don't you go ahead and do it? You can tell me all about it afterward."

"Since I'm only visiting, it wouldn't do me any good, but I'll go if you'll go. I'll be your wing-woman. We could ask Gigi to hold down the fort."

Being from out of town was a valid excuse. There was no sense in meeting men who lived in Savannah when she was in Atlanta. Then she wondered how long it would be before she was ready to put herself out there again. There'd been one guy, Heath Jordan, a high school chemistry teacher—sort of the mad scientist type. They'd dated for about six weeks, but then Elle had started feeling claustrophobic and called things off. There was no sense in hanging on if she saw no future. It was ironic that she couldn't find chemistry with a chemistry teacher. But she hadn't. In fact, the thought of sleeping with him—and running out of excuses why she wouldn't—was what had finally driven her away.

Chemistry was important.

And darn if her traitorous thoughts didn't rip right back to Daniel Quindlin and his broad shoulders. Her cheeks burned at the memory of seeing him in the park.

Okay, so the wedding—or the *almost* wedding—had been years ago. She wanted to believe she'd moved on, and until she'd seen Daniel, she'd believed she had. She wasn't pining over Roger. They hadn't talked in years. But if she was completely honest with herself, she still struggled with one burning question. Why had Daniel been so hell-bent on talking Roger out of marrying her? Even to the point that he'd nudged him to run out on her at the altar?

What had possessed Daniel to be so mean? But when

she'd pressed Roger for an explanation the one time they'd talked after the wedding, he'd told her he simply didn't love her enough to spend the rest of his life with her. That single stinging sentence was all she needed to know. She convinced herself that she didn't need Daniel's motive for pushing him. The bottom line was that Roger was the one who had made the choice to walk. As bitter as it was to swallow, it was probably the biggest favor anyone had ever done her.

That didn't mean she had to like Daniel Quindlin or let him taint her return to Savannah. Roger was long gone, a mere footnote in the annals of her life. The last she'd heard, he was in California. His parents had sold their home in Savannah and moved. There was no chance that she'd run into anyone from the Hathaway clan. While she was home, she'd steer clear of the places she might run into Daniel. As if they'd frequent the same places.

Inwardly, she rolled her eyes.

"Did you roll your eyes at me?" Zelda asked.

"What? No!" *Ugh, had she actually made that face?* "I have a lot on my mind. If I did, it wasn't directed at you. I'm sorry if you thought it was."

"Oh, honey, I know you've got a lot to sort out with your job. It sounds like everything will be okay. I'm sure it will sort itself out in the long run. We sure could use your help and we might even be able to pay you a little bit. I'm sure we could scare up the funds."

"No, Mom, I'm fine financially. I have savings. I'm sure it will be fine. But you know what? While I'm waiting for my reassignment, I could stay and help you and Gigi out. It seems like you could use an extra set of hands."

Zelda squealed and hugged Elle. "My middle baby girl is going to be home for the holidays. You know there is nothing in the world that makes me happier than having my girls home and I'm not sure Jane can get away from the restaurant long enough to come home this year. That's peak season for her. Oh, Elle, you couldn't give me a better Christmas present than being here. Just wait until I tell your Gigi. However, I'll pass on that speed dating. You and your sister Kate should go. The best thing you could do for yourself, missy, would be to start having fun again. The sooner the better."

No. Not the sooner the better. Zelda must've read it in her eyes, because she had a look on her face.

"What?" Elle asked. "Now you're the one making faces."

Zelda sighed and shook her head.

She thought about telling Zelda that she'd seen Daniel Quindlin in the park and asking her how long he'd been back in Savannah, but she didn't want to talk about him.

"Who's meeting here today?" Elle asked.

"The Savannah Women's Society. It's their monthly meeting. Only this one is special."

Ah, the esteemed *Society Ladies*, as everyone called them. She should've known.

For as far back as Elizabeth could remember, the Society Ladies had had a standing date at the Forsyth. They even had a dainty hand-painted announcement posted at the foot of the veranda steps, in fancy script:

*The Savannah Women's Society meets here the first
Saturday of every month except January and July. All
are welcome.*

"Really? How so?"

Zelda's eyes lit up. "Well, the hot topic on the agenda
is the group's annual benefit. You know how they award
a grant every year to fund a rehabilitation project in Savannah's historical district? Guess who is this year's
worthy recipient?"

Elizabeth shrugged. "I couldn't begin to guess."

"This year it's none other than the Forsyth Galloway
Inn." Zelda clapped her hands.

"Seriously? I didn't know they funded businesses
or private residences. I thought they'd stick to not-for-
profits."

"There are only so many statues and monuments
that need fixing. So they expanded to include all properties on the historical registry. The work we want to
do here is not just cosmetic. We're still doing repairs
after that tree uprooted and landed on the roof during
the last hurricane."

"Mom, the hurricane was several years ago. I thought
insurance covered the damage. Why haven't you fixed
it?"

"Well, insurance did give us some money for repairs,
but not nearly enough. Plus, you know how it is when
you fix up one thing—it makes everything else look
tired and shabby. It's like a domino chain. We fixed
the leak, but there wasn't enough money to replace the
wallpaper and refinish the floors where water warped
the boards and discolored the finish. Oh, well, there's a
whole long list of things that we need to do around here,

and you know how expensive repairs and renovations are. That's why we've been tightening our belts and doing a lot of the day-to-day upkeep ourselves. We applied for the Women's Society grant and we got it. The only problem is your Gigi and I have completely different visions of how the remodel should go. I'll have to tell you all about it later, after the meeting. We could use your voice of reason. But right now we need to finish getting things ready because this is the meeting when they're awarding the check. It's kind of a big deal."

"I'm so glad I could be here," Elle said, setting a bowl of fruit salad next to a tiered tray of scones and Danish pastries. "I hope they enjoy the breakfast."

"And to that end, I need to go check on the coffee. I just brewed some fresh. Want a cup?"

"No, thanks, I had a cup before I came down," Elizabeth said as she stepped back to admire their buffet handiwork. Everything was in its place. All they needed to do was fill the urn with coffee, and they'd be ready to welcome their guests.

After her mother left, Elizabeth glanced around the room, and saw for the first time its tired floral wallpaper and yellowing white wainscoting. In her mind's eye, the place had always been lovely. Now that Zelda had mentioned it, Elle could see what her mother meant about the decor being a little tired and in need of some love. In its day, the Forsyth had been the crowning glory of the neighborhood. Now the old girl resembled a grand dame who was showing her age. Yet, despite her wrinkles and sags, she still stood regal and proud, beloved by those like Elle, who cherished her timeless grace.

Maybe the Forsyth needed a little reno-Botox. Nothing invasive or reconstructive. Because the place was beautiful as she stood, wrinkles and all.

Elle's gaze snared the photos in silver frames on the wall and fireplace mantel. There were pictures of every ancestor who had lived here and managed the inn before her Gigi and mother. Someday she and her sisters would have their photos up there, too.

She took a deep breath and let the warmth of the memory of all those generations of independent, successful businesswomen—her people—wash over her. Coming home had been the right thing to do. It was a privilege to have such a birthright, a place like this to come home to when she needed to figure things out. She was happy to have the chance to help her mother and Gigi. After all, the best way to forget her problems was to be of service to someone else.

With a renewed sense of purpose, she left the dining room on a mission to fold the linens and deliver fresh towels to the Gibbons. She didn't get very far, because the first person she saw when she stepped out of the dining room was Daniel Quindlin.

Her heart did a sudden flip in her chest and the sensation had her hand fluttering to her throat.

He was standing in the lobby at the front desk, looking freshly showered and dressed after his run through the park. A crop of stubble had accumulated on his face, but not enough to be a beard.

Seeing him again up close made her remember that he was tall. How was it that today he seemed bigger and more menacing than she'd remembered? Maybe the sight of him there, invading her sanctuary, was making her feel fragile and vulnerable.

Well, she needed to get over it fast because she'd never considered herself breakable a single day in her life. She hadn't broken when Roger had left her at the altar, and she didn't intend to start now.

But Daniel loomed, dark and dangerous, like he'd come for her.

Self-preservation told her to turn around and hightail it back into the dining room, because she didn't want to talk to him. But it was too late; he'd already seen her.

Crap. She may or may not have uttered the oath out loud. She didn't care if she had. The only thing worse than seeing Daniel in the park this morning was getting a visit from the devil himself. He may have tried to steal her dignity, but he wasn't going to rob her of the comfort of coming home.

Chapter Two

"It's really you," Daniel said.

Elizabeth Clark raised her chin in that superior good-girl way she'd perfected when they were in high school.

"Were you expecting someone else?" Elle asked.

She was still sassy. And good God almighty, she was even more gorgeous than the last time he'd seen her standing there in that big white dress after Roger Hathaway had walked away from the best thing that would happen to his sorry life.

Since he'd seen her on the balcony, looking sexy and sleep rumpled, Elle had tamed her long blond hair back into a ponytail. That sweater she wore touched every curve in just the right place and made him wish he could, too.

"I was expecting you," he said. "I saw you this morning. I thought you waved at me."

She squinted at him and her nostrils flared, as if she smelled something as she looked down her perfect little nose at him. Her attitude made him want her more.

"I didn't realize you were in town until I saw you this morning up there on your balcony looking like Juliet." Since she was already rolling her eyes, he stopped himself before he offered to stand in as her Romeo. Besides, Romeo and Juliet died. Clearly, they weren't good for each other. "Don't you live in Atlanta now?"

"I didn't realize you were keeping track of me, Daniel."

"Don't worry, I'm not."

He smiled at her. She didn't smile back, but her cheeks turned a pretty shade of pink that matched her sweater.

"You just happen to know I'm living in Atlanta, but you're not keeping track. I see." She crossed her arms and a dainty hint of cleavage winked at him. He locked gazes with her to force his eyes to stay in respectable territory.

"I have no idea what you've been up to these days," she added. "I didn't know that you were back in town."

Her tone suggested she *didn't care* what he'd been up to or when he'd gotten back into town. He hadn't left Savannah under the best circumstances. And then there was the wedding-day incident, which she'd made perfectly clear she blamed on him. It was no wonder that she was surprised to see him. He'd always prided himself on bringing the element of surprise.

For the most part, Elle hadn't changed. Except that she was even prettier, but he wondered if that beauty came from an air of being a bit more self-possessed and worldly than she'd been. She wasn't a tough chick, but it seemed like she wouldn't put up with anyone's crap. Back in the day when she'd been with Roger, she was naive. That guy had a way of manipulating situations to make girlfriends believe he was faithful, parents think he was the Second Coming and friends eager to do his bidding.

Now Elle seemed sassier and maybe even just this side of jaded. Even though she'd been the quintessential good girl in high school—the cheerleader, the homecoming queen, the honor student, the artist—he'd always sensed a passionate side to her, lying dormant like a sleeping volcano that was waiting for the right man to stoke it. The thought of being the one to make the untouchable Elle Clark erupt was still his sexiest fantasy. And he had been around the block a few times.

"I live here now," he said. "My grandmother passed away a couple of years ago. My brother, Aidan, and I inherited her house over on Barnard Street. We run our business out of it. I rebuilt her place for her…after the accident."

The fire had been an accident. The unfortunate result of teenage boys with too much time on their hands and too little common sense to understand that certain fireworks were illegal for a reason. By the grace of God no one had been hurt, but his grandmother's house had been destroyed. Hell, if anything good had come of it, it had been his wake-up call. It had been the catalyst that had knocked the chip off his shoulder and made him start getting his act together.

"I heard about your grandmother's passing," Elle said, sympathy softening her blue, blue eyes. "I'm sorry."

He nodded his thanks and shoved his hands in the back pockets of his jeans, wracking his brain for something else to say.

"How's life in Atlanta?" he asked, wanting to keep the conversation going. Her blue eyes darkened a shade and she bit her full bottom lip. He wondered if her mouth still tasted as sweet as it had all those years ago—

"Life in Atlanta is fine, thank you." Elizabeth's brow furrowed. Her expression and clipped words hinted that might not be the truth...or maybe she'd read his mind. "Thanks for stopping by. May I help you with something else?"

A list of ways that she could *help* him—such as finishing what they'd started back in the day, before Roger horned in—pinged through his head, but good sense kept the request from falling off his tongue.

"Not today. I'm here to see your grandmother." He nodded toward Wiladean Boudreau, who was descending the big staircase that spilled into the lobby. "But thanks, anyway. I'll let you know if I think of something."

"Oh." He couldn't tell if Elle was more surprised by his meeting with Wiladean or his comment. He hoped it was a little of both.

Elle's head turned in the direction of her grandmother, who was now walking toward them.

"Actually, I did think of something," he said. "Want to grab a drink sometime while you're home?"

Slim chance. But one thing he'd learned over the past few years was if you didn't ask, the answer was always no.

* * *

"Well, good," Gigi said. "Good! I'm glad you two have had a chance to say hello." There was a certain gleam in her grandmother's eye that made Elle uncomfortable. "If you didn't run into each other this morning, I was going to make sure Daniel knew you were home. So you two could get reacquainted."

Gigi's eyes glinted with mischief, but the way she was surreptitiously glancing around the lobby didn't escape Elle's notice. "But right now, you'll have to excuse us, Elle, dear. Daniel and I have some business to discuss."

"What kind of business, Gigi?" Gigi's entrance had provided a reason to pretend like Daniel hadn't asked her out for a drink, but it was eclipsed by the fact that he was there to see her grandmother. "Did you forget the breakfast meeting with the Society Ladies is this morning?"

Wiladean's gaze flitted toward the dining room, where the women were beginning to arrive, and then back to Elizabeth and Daniel. "No, I didn't forget. But now that you mention it, why don't you go help your mother greet everyone, dear? I'm sure they'll be delighted to see you." She motioned for Daniel to follow her. "This shouldn't take very long."

As Gigi and Daniel started walking toward the office, Elizabeth said, "I'm happy to help Mom, but before I do, I'd like to know what your meeting with Daniel is about."

She directed the words to Daniel, whose stoic expression didn't give up anything.

Usually, she wouldn't have gotten into Gigi's business like this, but her grandmother was acting squirrelly, and this was *Daniel Quindlin*. He was good-looking and charming and the last person on earth she'd trust alone with anyone she cared about, especially Gigi. Something was going on and she intended to get to the bottom of it.

Wiladean laughed. "Bless your heart, Elle. You've always been too curious for your own good."

She raised her brows at her grandmother.

"Gigi," Elle said, using her best teacher's voice.

"Oh, honey, Daniel is here to talk about some renovations we want to do to the place." She shrugged and waved her hand, as if the reason for the meeting should've been perfectly obvious. "That's all."

"Why are you talking to *Daniel* about the remodel?"

What kind of a racket was he trying to pull? *And on my Gigi?*

"I'm a licensed general contractor." To Daniel's credit, he didn't sound defensive. "I specialize in restoring old houses like this one. It's what I do."

Elle recalled that he'd said he'd rebuilt his grandmother's house after the fire, and he had worked construction jobs when they were in high school. Sometimes he'd skipped school to take day labor jobs for extra money. That was why he'd gotten behind in school and she'd had to tutor him.

Well, for one day, anyway.

Then he'd kissed her and she'd freaked out and she'd told the principal she was too busy to help him. And she was. She was dating Roger. Plus, she was a straight A honor student, student body president, head of the art club and chair of the honor society tutoring committee.

Backing out on helping the new kid bring up his grades hadn't looked good, but Daniel had scared her to death. Because when he'd kissed her, she'd kissed him back. That one kiss had made her feel things and want to do things she'd never realized she was capable of feeling or doing. Things a good girl didn't feel or do. Roger had certainly never made her feel like that. Daniel was dark and dangerous. When she'd looked into his brown eyes, she sensed that he'd already lived a thousand lives and bore scars from each one.

When he'd befriended Roger, she'd always felt like that kiss was blackmail material.

From that point forward she'd never trusted Daniel Quindlin.

"Why does your meeting have to take place at the same time that the Savannah Women's Society is about to present you with a check? You should be in that meeting, not this one."

"Oh, go on now and stop being so bossy," Gigi said. "I'm the queen bee around here, missy, and I'm asking you to go help your mama with the breakfast and leave us to our meeting."

"Okay, I'll go help Mom. I'll tell her you asked me to fill in for you because you're meeting with Daniel."

"Now, don't do that. Don't you say anything to her." Urgency was plain as day in Gigi's forced smile.

"Why not?" Elle recalled her mother saying that the two of them had been at an impasse over the remodeling project. "Gigi, are you meeting with Daniel on the sly?"

Wiladean sighed and fixed Elizabeth with a pointed look. "Elle, dear, don't be silly. I don't have time to explain things right now, but I will fill both you and your mother in on the details later."

Wiladean smiled and waved at someone Elizabeth didn't recognize. The woman started walking in their direction.

"This is exactly why I need your help," Gigi said under her breath, keeping her smile intact. "If I don't get out of here, I'll get pulled into the Society Ladies' meeting."

Elle raised her brows, conveying the message she wasn't going anywhere until Gigi fessed up.

"Your mom and I are having… Oh, how do I say it? Zelda and I are having creative differences and we are at a standoff with the direction of the renovation. We have different visions for the inn and I wanted to talk to Daniel alone." Wiladean lowered her voice another decibel as the other woman approached. "Will you help me, please?"

Before Elizabeth could answer, Gigi's friend approached.

"Wiladean, the Forsyth looks lovely as always. Though I imagine our grant will help you fix that unsightly water damage."

As the woman bent in and blew air kisses onto each of Gigi's cheeks, her gaze was shamelessly pinned on Daniel. Elizabeth slanted a look at her former classmate, who, as much as Elle hated to admit it, was looking particularly good this morning—every tall, lean, darkly handsome inch of him. Who could blame the woman for looking, even if she was old enough to be his grandmother?

Daniel seemed oblivious.

It struck Elizabeth that there was a time when most of polite Savannah society didn't want anything to do with him. My, how times had changed. This woman was looking at him like she wanted to eat him for breakfast.

"Wiladean, would you like to reschedule?" he asked. "This seems like it's a bad time."

"No, Daniel," Gigi insisted.

"Oh, is this *the* Daniel Quindlin?" the other woman asked. She sounded a little too coy.

Gigi nodded.

"I'm Angela Stanton." The woman offered her diamond-laden hand. Daniel shook it. "I've heard so much about you, but I haven't had the pleasure. You are in demand, young man. Perhaps I could schedule a time to talk to you about remodeling my home. I'm right around the corner on Monterey Square. I bought the place after my husband passed away."

The hungry, grieving widow. Of course.

"Angela, you remodeled six months ago—if that," Gigi said. "What more could you have to do?"

"It's a never-ending job, Wiladean," Angela said. "You of all people should know." She turned to Elizabeth. "And who is this lovely creature?"

"This is my middle granddaughter, Elizabeth. Elle arrived from Atlanta last night. She surprised us. We're so happy to have her home. She is going to attend the meeting on my behalf this morning."

"Aren't you a pretty thing," Angela gushed.

"Thank you," Elle said. She could feel the burn of Daniel's gaze on her. "It's nice to meet you, Mrs. Stanton."

"Are you married?" the woman asked. "If not, the

two of you would make a lovely couple. Wouldn't they make the most beautiful babies, Willa?"

Elle flinched. She hoped her discomfort wasn't as obvious as it felt. Right about now, she felt beet red at the thought of having beautiful babies with Daniel. She couldn't even look at him.

"I'm certainly not going to dispute that," said Gigi. "I'm almost eighty-five years old. At this age, my only goal is for one of my grandgirls to get married and make me a great-Gigi." She eyed Daniel and Elle. "I have plans for these two."

For the love of all things mortifying.

Was she kidding?

"Uh-oh, there's Zelda," Gigi said. "Daniel, go into the office. Quickly."

Thank heaven for diversions. Elle nearly crumbled under the awkwardness of her grandmother and Angela talking about mating her and Daniel—the person who was responsible for ruining her marriage—as if they were two show dogs.

For that matter, why was Gigi consorting with the enemy? Even if Angela had said he was in demand as a contractor, it didn't matter. Builders in this area had to be a dime a dozen. It wasn't as if they were doing major construction to the inn. She'd talk to Gigi about that later and it would probably be a good idea to have a little talk about boundaries. She had not come home to be fixed up with the guy who had ruined her life.

Gigi stepped in front of Daniel as if her slight frame could hide him. "Go," she said. "I'll be along shortly."

But it was to no avail.

"Daniel?" Zelda said. "What are you doing here this morning?"

Zelda looked pointedly at her mother as if she sensed something was rotten.

"He stopped by to talk about the renovation," Wiladean said.

"I'll leave y'all to sort out this matter," said Angela. "I see Bunny Henry over there and I need to chat with her." With a flutter of her fingers, gaze scanning the room, Angela disengaged from the conversation.

Zelda looked skeptical. "Isn't that nice, Daniel. But it's just about the worst time imaginable. Isn't it, Mother? We are hosting the Savannah Women's Society this morning. Could you possibly come back this afternoon?"

So, wait. Was her mother in on hiring Daniel for the remodel, too? Seriously?

"I have to be at another jobsite this afternoon," he said. "But I could swing by later this morning." He looked at his watch. "Maybe around ten? Would you be free then?"

Maybe she was jumping the gun. Maybe they hadn't hired him yet and this was a courtesy interview? *Humph.* Daniel Quindlin deserved the same courtesy he'd shown her when he'd nudged her fiancé to make a run for it.

Elizabeth waited for the rat to correct Gigi, to tell Zelda he hadn't *dropped by unannounced*, that Gigi had obviously scheduled their secret rendezvous well in advance. For that matter, that she'd intended for it to happen while Zelda was busy facilitating the Savannah Women's Society this morning.

But he didn't dispute her. He stood there and kept Gigi's secret.

"Why don't you both talk to Daniel while the ladies are eating their breakfast, and I'll keep an eye on everything in the dining room," Elizabeth said. "The hard part is done, right? All I'll need to do is restock the food as it gets low, refill water glasses and be available if anyone needs anything. I'll let you know when they're ready to start the meeting and you both can be there for the presentation of the check. I mean, you're not looking at blueprints or choosing finishings at this point, are you?"

She knew Gigi wouldn't be very happy with her for offering a solution that would free up Zelda to meet with Daniel, but Gigi hadn't exactly been playing fair, either.

This would level the playing field.

She'd handled meetings and parties like this hundreds of times when she was in high school and living at the Forsyth.

"Thank you, honey, but I don't think so." Zelda took off her apron, folded it and draped it over her arm. "The Women's Society is giving us money. It seems rude not to join them for breakfast. It's as if we're taking the money and running. That would be ungrateful, wouldn't it, Mother? I'm sorry, Daniel, but we need to reschedule for later this morning. You're awfully sweet to accommodate us."

Gigi frowned. "I think you need to be in that breakfast meeting, Zelda. You and Elle. You're the next generations who will run the Forsyth. I'll be retiring pretty soon and you'll be running the show."

"That's more reason I should have input on the remodel," Zelda said. "Come on, Mother. Let's not get into it now. All three of us need to be in there for the Savannah Women's Society meeting. Three generations of Galloway-Boudreau-Clark women. Let's go welcome everyone."

Elizabeth could sense the argument perched behind Gigi's pursed lips, ready to pounce. But when Zelda turned and started walking toward the dining room, Gigi sighed and followed her daughter, leaving Elle alone with Daniel.

"Welcome home, Elle. Let's figure out when we're going to get that drink."

Her mind screamed *no, thank you*, but damned if her traitorous heart didn't leap at the thought.

Later that morning, Daniel ran into Elle again after he'd finished meeting with Zelda and Wiladean. Elle had not been invited to join them. However, both Zelda and Wiladean had been armed with plenty of big, opposing opinions.

"How did it go?" she asked tentatively.

She was seated at the mahogany bar that served as a front desk and a general repository for pamphlets, brochures and other touristy info. He'd sensed her presence the spilt second before she'd spoken. Yep, he still had a sort of sixth sense when it came to Elizabeth Clark. It was as if his body was hardwired to detect her.

He smiled, trying to buy time so he could come up with a diplomatic answer. Something more professional than "Talk about being caught between a rock and a hard place" or "That was a no-win meeting."

"Your mom and grandmother definitely have their

own ideas about the remodel and they're about one hundred and eighty degrees apart from each other. I thought maybe you'd be in the meeting. To moderate. No offense to those in attendance."

He wasn't going to tell Elle that he'd suggested they call him after they'd come to a meeting of the minds. Because until they did, meetings like this were a waste of everyone's time. Of course, since Wiladean was the one with the checkbook, she would likely have the last word. However, Zelda had made it clear the grant from the Savannah Women's Society belonged to all of them and she wasn't giving up on her vision anytime soon.

It wasn't his call to play referee. He would build and refurbish whatever they told him to do. But they had to have a plan.

"The Galloway-Boudreau-Clark women never have been short on opinions," she said. "Since I wasn't invited to the meeting, it wasn't my place to insert myself. I'm sure they'll figure it out. So, you're a contractor now?"

He nodded. "I specialize in rehabbing old houses in the historic and Victorian districts."

"I know you worked construction when we were in school, but how did you get into that specialization?"

She remembered.

Her brows were knitted and she was smiling as if she were waiting for him to deliver the punchline to a joke. He supposed he might still be a joke in her eyes. But he was good at what he did. That was why he was getting so much business he was having to refer people elsewhere or put them on a waiting list. Most opted for the waiting list.

He wasn't going to tell Elizabeth this, because he didn't need to explain himself.

Instead, he pulled out his wallet, took out a business card and handed it to her.

She looked at it and read aloud. "'Quindlin Brothers Renovations—Saving Savannah one historic house at a time.'" Then she looked back at him.

"Professional."

"I do my best."

"I'm sure you do."

Her eyes were still as blue as he remembered. Bluer than the Savannah sky on a clear winter day. He could get lost in those eyes. But over the past several years, he'd worked hard to grow his business to this point and earn the respect of the people in the community. The last thing he needed to do was mess around and screw things up so that it affected the job Wiladean had hired him to do at the inn. Elle's grandmother had always been kind to him. She'd taken in his grandmother and brother after the fire, giving them a place to stay; she'd been one of the first people to forget the sins of his youth and offer good words when people asked for a character reference. Now she'd hired him to renovate her own home and business.

Even though his business was flourishing, if he offended Wiladean Galloway-Boudreau, he'd stand to lose a lot of business. He'd made some bad choices in his life, but he had no intention of messing up now.

Chapter Three

When Elle wheeled the last cart of dirty dishes from the Women's Society meeting into the kitchen, her mother was at the sink, washing the delicate china cups and setting each aside. Elle parked the cart, picked up the dish towel and began drying.

"How was the meeting with Daniel?" Elle asked.

Zelda sighed. "Your grandmother and I are at a stand-off."

"What is this all about? Why can't you two agree?"

"It's the age-old struggle she and I have always had. She wants things to stay the same. I want change. I need change."

No surprise there.

Elle slanted a glance at her mother. "What kind of change are you talking about?"

That was the burning question. The Forsyth Galloway Inn had been mostly the same since the family had started the business in 1874. Maybe not exactly the same, as the mansion had originally been built to serve as the Galloway family's home, but over the years they'd stuck to variations on a traditional theme.

Zelda looked thoughtful as she rinsed the cup she'd washed, handed it to Elizabeth and dried her hands on her apron.

"Don't you get tired of things always being the same?"

Elle blinked at her mother.

The question went against her grain. As an art teacher, she had lessons to plan, classes to teach, projects to grade and supplies to order. She lived by herself, but she had friends and a book club and she did volunteer work, as well as grocery shopping, meal planning and prep and house maintenance. Routine was the only thing that allowed her to keep all the balls she juggled in the air.

A sharp pang pierced her gut as she remembered that the main thing that kept her so busy—her job—had been crossed off the list. She was unemployed until further notice.

"Oh, I don't know," she said, placing the cup in line with the others on the trestle table in the middle of the large kitchen. "Sometimes sameness can be…comforting."

Zelda scoffed. "Sameness is a prison. No, I take that back. Sameness is a death sentence. Sameness is a— Elle, are you crying? What's wrong, honey?"

Ugggh.

Elle looked up at the ceiling, trying in vain to blink

back the tears. She'd promised herself she wouldn't do this. She didn't even know where the tears came from. She'd almost convinced herself that all these changes that were being foisted on her were for the best. But now it suddenly felt as if the rug had been pulled out from under her.

Her mother was at her side, putting her arms around Elizabeth, pulling her in for a hug.

Zelda held her like that for a few minutes, patting Elle's back, before saying. "Sweetie, it's going to be okay. I'm going to make us a pot of tea and I want you to talk to me."

Zelda tore a paper towel off the roll and handed it to her. Elle blew her nose and sat down on a bench at the trestle table.

Her mother put the kettle on and joined her at the table. "What's going on, honey?"

"The situation with my job is a bit worse than I let on last night."

Zelda nodded. "I wondered about that."

"Why? Was it obvious?"

"No. On the contrary. You've been pretty stoic since you got home last night. Even so, it didn't escape my mom-radar that something wasn't right."

As Elle filled in the details she'd left out last night, about how she could be unemployed for the better part of the year, her mother nodded along sympathetically.

The kettle whistled. She squeezed Elle's hand and got up to brew the pot.

"Earl Grey or Darjeeling?"

"Let's visit with the Earl," Elle said. "I've got the cups." She reached over and claimed two of the pretty china cups they'd washed and dried. Zelda returned with the white teapot with pink roses. That teapot held so many memories. When she and her sisters were growing up, anytime there was a problem or a celebration, their mom would put on the kettle and brew tea in that same pot.

Boy, the stories it could tell if it could talk.

Elle smiled at the thought.

Zelda set the pot on the table, turned over the tea timer and set to work putting together a plate of cinnamon scones that were left over from the breakfast. There wasn't much a perfectly brewed cup of tea and a good scone couldn't cure. The sight of the comfort snack on the table between them warmed Elle from the inside out.

As they waited for the tea to steep, they helped themselves to the scones.

"Is there any chance that they'd hire you to teach art at another school?" Zelda asked.

Elizabeth shrugged. "Not until next fall. Unless an art teacher quits during the next semester. Art teacher jobs are rare since they're electives and the county has slashed the budget. Our school foundation was funding my position for the short-term, with hopes that the county would make room for it in the budget. My principal is trying to place me somewhere doing something else, but she can't make any promises."

"If they can place you what would they want you to do?"

"Teach an elementary grade or possibly work as a reading or curriculum support staff."

"The teaching might not be bad, but the other makes my eyes glaze over just thinking about it," Zelda said.

Elizabeth frowned at her mother, and Zelda held up her hands in surrender.

"I know, I know. They're important jobs, very honorable jobs, but Elle, I can't see you being happy planning curriculum."

Elizabeth shrugged. "I wouldn't mind teaching, though."

"But would you love it?"

"I love kids. You know I do."

"But would you really want to get roped into doing something your heart really wasn't in?"

"Mom, I have to make a living."

"I know you do," Zelda said. "But what about your art? You're so talented. Teaching art took you away from making your own art, but at least you were still immersed in helping kids be creative. Maybe this is the universe's way of telling you something? That you need to focus on your own creativity."

"Mom, you know how difficult it is to make a living as an artist. That's why I went the teaching route."

"And what have you created in the past six years since you started teaching?"

She was right. After Elle spent so much time planning and grading art projects and papers for the kids, working on her own painting was really the last thing she wanted to do in her limited spare time. Since the wedding fell through, she'd all but abandoned her own art, except for the occasional page she did in her art journal.

Zelda leaned in and placed her folded hands on the table. "Hear me out, okay? What if I knew of a way for you to work as an artist and make money?"

Elle sipped her tea, trying not to look too skeptical before she heard her mother out. Zelda was one of Elle's favorite people in the world. She was a great mother, always there for Elle when she needed her. Like right now, which was why instinct had guided Elle home in her moment of crisis. But at the same time, Zelda wasn't always the most practical person. In her quiet way, she was often flighty and free-spirited, both traits that Elle loved about her mother but also made her dubious about taking career advice from her.

She swallowed the sip of tea and set her cup back on the saucer. She took care to infuse a smile into her voice before looking at her mother and saying, "What do you have in mind?"

Zelda's green eyes lit up. "I want to turn the inn into a Zen-based artists' retreat."

She beamed. Elle blinked at her.

She didn't have to hear any more to connect the dots. This was the crux of Zelda and Wiladean's redesign stalemate. It had to be.

"Is Gigi on board with this idea?"

Zelda swatted the air as if she was shooing away Elle's question. She sat back and crossed her arms.

"You know that your grandmother and I have very different visions for the direction of the inn," Zelda said. "We're investing a pretty penny into this renovation and I think she should be more open-minded. She's talking about retiring this year and signing the inn over to me. She says she doesn't want me to have to wait for her to die before I get my turn running the place." Zelda frowned. "I appreciate that, but don't you think she should let me run the inn my way?"

"And your way is turning the place into a Zen-based artists' retreat?"

Zelda nodded. "Doesn't that sound wonderful? Come on, Elle, you're an artist, you should see the beauty in it."

"Mom, I'm not taking sides," Elle said. "But don't you think that's a pretty far departure from the Forsyth Galloway Inn's legacy?"

"But Elle, you *should* take sides. This is your birthright, too. You're an artist. I thought you'd be excited about us offering artists' retreats."

Elle sensed that she was about to step onto a minefield. All she needed was for her mother to tell Wiladean that Elle was on board with the artists' retreats. Elle was intrigued, but it was a big leap away from how their ancestors had always done things, miles away from the centuries-old business model on which they'd built their modest success.

"I'm not taking sides," Elle said. "But I would like to hear what you have in mind."

Zelda smiled and sat forward again. "I was thinking of ways that we could set ourselves apart from the hundreds of bed-and-breakfasts in this town and, poof, it came to me. Savannah is an artistic community. Offering a place for people with artistic sensibilities to stay and create while they're here would not only be different, but it could be a big draw—pardon the pun." She chuckled and looked proud of herself for the clever play on words. Then she reached out and touched Elle's arm. "Think about it. We could organize art-themed excursions and programs. We could turn the dining room, with all those beautiful windows and all that glorious light, into an open studio where people could draw and paint. We could hold classes out in the garden and turn one of the detached guesthouses into a classroom. Here's the best part—you could teach those classes."

"Mom, I'm an elementary school art teacher."

"Stop selling yourself short, Elle. You're a talented artist. People would pay good money to take classes from you. Plus, you're a native daughter of Savannah and a graduate of SCAD. I'll bet the college would partner with us."

"Mom, the college has no shortage of guest lodging. I mean, Magnolia Hall is right down the street."

"Yes, but as far as I know it's only for visiting artists and people here on official college business. We could cater to a segment of the market that's not being served."

She had a point. It was an opportunity to grasp an underserved section of the tourism population.

"Why is Gigi so opposed to the idea?"

Zelda waved her hand in the air again. "She can't get past the Zen part."

Elizabeth should've known. Gigi was as traditional as a Sunday roast.

"I'd also like to offer spa services and yoga classes. And tea." Zelda held up her cup. "How fun would it be to get Daniel Quindlin to build us a little tearoom?"

It happened again. Elle's stomach did another flip at the mention of Daniel's name. Only this time it was an extended version with a little stutter step at the end. She put her hand on her stomach to calm the ridiculous feeling.

"Maybe Jane would even come home and run a tearoom for us," Zelda mused.

Elizabeth's sister Jane was a pastry chef and was living her dream in New York City. She was in charge of desserts at celebrity chef Liam Wright's über-hot restaurant, La Bula. Jane's star was on the rise. Fat chance she'd leave the big time to come home and open a tearoom in a bed-and-breakfast with an identity crisis.

"Honestly, Mom, you had my attention when you were talking art, but adding the spa and tearoom seems like you're muddying the waters a bit. Is it a spa or an artists' retreat?"

Zelda raised her chin. "I want it all, Elle. Why can't I have it all?"

Wasn't that the age-old question? Didn't everyone want it all? Whatever *all* was.

"I'm not saying you can't have it all, but you're courting two different markets with the spa and art retreat."

Suddenly it hit her.

"Would you ask Kate to run the spa?"

"If I had my girls here to run the place with me, life would be just about as perfect as it could get. And to me, that's the definition of having it all. I mean, the three of you will inherit the place after I'm gone…or after I sign it over to you. You'll carry on the family legacy. I can't think of a better way for y'all to learn the business."

Zelda looked so hopeful, sitting there with her wide green eyes and her soft auburn curls framing her pretty face and falling around her slight shoulders, that Elizabeth hated to be the one to give her a reality check.

"Have you talked to Jane and Kate about your plan?"

"Well, no. Not yet. I wanted to bounce it off you first. You've always been the voice of reason around here. And I wanted to come to a meeting of the minds with

Gigi before I did that. But she's being so difficult. Elle, will you help me? Will you help me convince her that this is a good idea?"

The problem was, Elle didn't know if it was a good idea. Even though the Forsyth Galloway Inn was desperately in need of a good facelift, the old girl was still 85 percent booked until after the first of the year. There was obviously a market for traditional bed-and-breakfasts in Savannah. Maybe they shouldn't mess with a good thing?

"So, did you mention any of this in the meeting with Daniel Quindlin?"

Zelda toyed with the scone she had been picking at since they sat down. Finally, she looked up and shook her head. "We didn't get to the point of talking specifics because Gigi and I can't seem to agree on anything. To tell you the truth, I think Daniel left feeling a bit frustrated."

Oh, he had. Elizabeth recalled the conversation and the strange, flustered breathless way she'd felt when she was talking to him. Certainly not the way that most women would act around the guy who'd caused them to get dumped.

Yes, that was what she needed to remind herself when Daniel Quindlin's handsome face made her stomach go all fluttery. *He ruined your wedding. He ruined your life.* Okay, so that was a little dramatic. But not so long ago, he'd disliked her so much that he'd urged Roger to break it off.

One could argue that the only reason he was being polite now was because of the work he'd been contracted to do on the inn.

"Maybe you should put the renovation on hold until you have a better idea of what you want to do."

"Absolutely not," Zelda insisted. "Every day that we haven't established our new identity is a day that we lose business."

"Maybe so," Elizabeth said.

But every day that they held off on the renovation would be a day without Daniel Quindlin in her personal space while she was trying to figure out what she would do next.

"Can I ask you something?"

"Sure, honey. Anything."

"Why did you hire Daniel?"

Zelda answered with a bemused smile. "Why not?"

"He's always had a reputation for not being the most reliable person. You know, after everything that happened with his grandmother and her house."

And the wedding. Did everyone get amnesia in the tractor beam of Daniel's smile?

Elle sipped her tea, which had cooled to room temperature.

"Oh, Elizabeth, that was so long ago. He was just a kid. People change as they grow up. You of all people should know how important it is for people to not hold past mistakes against people."

She choked on her tea and coughed as she tried to talk. "What is that supposed to mean? What have I done other than trust the wrong man with my heart? You know, scratch that. It's a good thing that we *didn't* get married, because that would mean that I'd married the wrong man. So, I don't care what other people think, Mom. I mean, we're not living in the Victorian era."

"Well, I was using that as a contrast. People grow and change. Just like you've grown and changed. He has cultivated quite the clientele around here. He does great work. He's quite sought after for renovations of old houses like this."

"But does he do Zen? I really don't remember that being on the menu of historic Savannah properties. Somehow, I think that tips the power in Gigi's favor."

"That's not fair, Elizabeth." Her mother only called her Elizabeth when she was mad at her or frustrated or the conversation was serious. "He's a good guy, but I don't want to talk about him."

Good. I don't, either.

"How did we get off the subject of you, Jane, Kate and me running the place together?"

"Running the place? We weren't talking about the four of us running the place...only helping out. Gigi is running the place. And then you'll run the place."

Zelda nodded and didn't answer Elle's question.

"Well, Gigi needs to know that regardless of how she renovates, when it's my turn to run the inn, I'm going through with the changes I have in mind. It would be a shame to waste money."

As much as Elle didn't want to take sides, her mother had a point. If Gigi wanted to retire, she should set up Zelda to run the place the way she wanted. In the meantime, maybe they could reach a happy medium that would work for both of them.

Yes, it might work...

"You know, you may be onto something, Mom. Maybe you and Gigi could meet in the middle. Let her keep the interior and exterior of the inn true to its roots, and give the new art focus a trial run while I'm home. We could do a test and see how an art class is received. I know you're already mostly booked through next year, but you could advertise a class and I could put together some local art tours and start getting the word out. Maybe you'll be able to fill the fifteen percent vacancy and maximize profits?"

Zelda hopped up and threw her arms around Elle. "I knew I could count on you to see the big picture. Will you please talk to Gigi about it? She will listen to you, sweetie."

The next morning, Daniel parked his truck on Hall Street, the road that ran along the south side of the Forsyth Galloway Inn. Wiladean had called and said they were ready to give him clear marching orders as to the direction of the remodel. She wanted to sit down with him and lay out everything. He wanted to get the project started. Even though she'd requested the meeting at short notice, he was happy to rearrange some things to fit her in.

He still felt beholden to Wiladean for taking such good care of his grandmother and brother, letting them stay at the inn after the house had burned down. Others in town weren't so nice about it. While the years had taught him to let go of anger and not hold grudges, he'd never forgotten those who were kind to him and his family when they were in need.

Now he was in a position to repay their kindness. Ironically, the very fire that had driven him out of town, causing him to leave school abruptly and forcing him to get his GED rather than graduating from high school, had been the very thing that had built his business. While he was away, he had worked construction and perfected his trade. When he came back, he'd rebuilt his grandmother's house and made damn sure not only to leave the nineteenth century Victorian in better condition than it had been before the fire, but to restore it to its glorious historical splendor. He'd researched the hell out of houses of that period and painstakingly tracked down original doors and windows, trim and moldings, among other fixtures that were true to that era.

The result had not only made his grandma proud, it had made her a minor celebrity in a town where old looking new and true again was held in the highest regard. Wiladean had been his first client, when she'd hired him to do some minor repairs. That job had snowballed into the business he'd built with his architect brother, Aidan.

Tablet in hand, he entered through the inn's front doors. Reflexively, his gaze went to the front desk, hoping to find Elle exactly where he'd left her yesterday. A man and woman, who he assumed were guests, were perusing the pamphlets, but Elle wasn't there. His hopes did an odd nosedive. As he was trying to reconcile the peculiar feeling, Wiladean stepped out of the office.

"Right on time," she said, glancing at her watch. "I do appreciate a man who is punctual."

He smiled at her. "Good morning, Wiladean."

"Come on into the office." She motioned for him to follow her. "We don't want to keep you very long since you were so kind to meet with us this morning on such short notice. I hope you don't mind, but Elle is going to sit in on the meeting. We have her to thank for Zelda and me coming to a meeting of the minds."

He wasn't surprised about that, but what did surprise him was the level of anticipation he felt as he walked toward the office door. He tried to tell himself that it was just relief that Wiladean and Zelda had finally come to an agreement. But the visceral reaction he experienced as he walked in and saw Elle sitting there looking fresh-faced and gorgeous made him realize he was in trouble. It was one thing to appreciate her from afar but another to…anticipate. He didn't do anticipation. Or at least he should know better than getting too attached to the idea of seeing her, because he couldn't have her, and he needed to get that through his head right now.

She'd piled her long, blond hair into a bun on top of her head. She wore a simple blue T-shirt and faded jeans. She looked even prettier than she had yesterday in that sweater with her hair and makeup done. He liked this more natural look. Not that it mattered, because he shouldn't be thinking about her appearance. This was business.

"Morning," he said.

The corners of Elle's lips tipped up into a half smile. "Good morning."

He started to sit in the chair closest to the door, but Wiladean said, "Move down, Daniel. Take the seat next to Elle."

"Let Daniel sit wherever he wants, Gigi," Elle quipped. Her tone was light, but Daniel sensed something else. "Do you remember what we talked about yesterday? Daniel, yesterday I asked Gigi to stop trying to push us together. It's fine if we want to work together, but I told her we have boundaries. Right, Gigi?"

"Don't you start with me, missy," Wiladean said. "Your mother is getting some coffee and muffins ready for us. Quarters are tight because this office wasn't really meant for four people. We don't need her maneuvering around us with hot coffee. By the way, Daniel, did Elle tell you she's decided to spend the holidays in Savannah to help us with a project she and Zelda came up with?"

Elle sighed. "When would I have had the chance to tell him that, Gigi? I just told you last night." Elle stood up. "I'm going to see if Mom needs any help in the kitchen."

Elle stood, but Wiladean beat her to the doorway. "You two visit and I'll go help Zelda."

"Visit?" Elle said. "Gigi, Daniel didn't come to visit—"

"You're absolutely right. Elle, you go ahead and tell Daniel about the new plan and I'll go hurry up your mother. I'll be right back."

She was gone in a flash, leaving the two of them alone in an awkward silence.

Elle sat back in her chair and crossed her arms over her chest, looking less than thrilled to be stuck in the tiny office with him.

"So, you're staying in Savannah for a bit?"

"Apparently so."

When Daniel had first come back to Savannah and tried to talk to people about his new business, he'd faced similar chilliness to what he was getting from Elle. Many remembered him and tried to brand him as an eternal troublemaker, someone not to be trusted. He'd found the best way to break through their barriers was to keep talking, asking questions about nonthreatening, inconsequential subjects that forced them to answer him. One thing about Southerners was that they wouldn't be caught dead being intentionally rude. They specialized in the veiled insult that made the uninitiated scratch his or her head wondering if they'd been complimented or damned. He had decided he would keep making polite conversation until they walked away or realized he wasn't such a bad guy after all. That was exactly what he planned to do now.

"What made you decide to stay?" he asked.

She gazed at him for a moment and drew her bottom lip between her teeth. Damned if his body didn't respond to the lip bite, that old familiar fallback defense gesture of hers.

He wanted to bite her bottom lip himself. He wanted to suck on it and draw it into his mouth and see if it still tasted as good as he remembered from all those years ago when he'd kissed her.

"If I don't stay, Gigi and Mom might kill each other. Or at the very least they'll keep fighting over the specifics of the renovation and y'all will get nothing done. I can't have that on my conscience."

There it was. She was talking to him. That was progress.

He turned in his chair so that he was facing her straight on. "So, I have you to thank for getting this project ready to roll?"

"I don't know about that."

"Need a job? Maybe I should hire you on as my project manager?"

She got a funny look on her face, but it only lasted a fleeting moment. She raised her chin. "I didn't realize you were hiring. Don't you have a regular crew?"

There was an edge to her voice, but he was beginning to like brushing up against her sharp edges. He liked this confidence she had now. It was sexy. She'd become a stronger woman, not the timid good girl she was in high school. And when she'd almost married Roger.

"For the record, I'm not hiring," he said. "But I could find a place for you if you wanted to come *on board*." Her cheeks turned that particular shade of pink that looked so good on her. It belied her bravado and made him believe that a little bit of the good girl had made it through the years unscathed. He felt a muscle in his jaw twitch. He should tone it down if he knew what was good for him. But flirting with her felt too damn good to resist. "Are you interested, Elle?"

She scowled at him, and for a moment, she looked as if she wanted to say something. Electricity virtually crackled between them, and judging by the look on her face, she felt it, too. But then again, the push-pull of unrequited attraction had never been their problem. Quite the contrary. This feeling that pulsed like a living, breathing thing was still there. Even if she wouldn't acknowledge it. "I'm not interested in anything permanent in Savannah."

"Good to know," he said. "Who says it needs to be permanent?"

"You don't want to try and go down that road with me, Daniel," Elle said.

Oh, yes, he did. And even though her words said one thing, her eyes telegraphed something else. He was trying to give her something to grab onto—a starting point for them—but it was clear that she was messing with him. This was a business meeting. He needed to reel it in a bit.

That was fine. Savannah wasn't built in a day. He'd waited years for her. He could wait a little bit longer.

"Tell me about this meeting of the minds you helped Zelda and Wiladean reach."

Elle's face softened and she sat forward in her chair. "You already know that they have two different remodel styles in mind."

Daniel nodded.

"Two ideas that are at opposite ends of the spectrum," he added.

Elle shrugged. "I asked Zelda why she wanted something so radically different from the way the Forsyth has always been and came to find out she doesn't really mind the traditional style of the inn as much as she wants to make changes so that we can expand the amenities we offer."

That was interesting. It was something they hadn't touched on in previous meetings.

"What kind of amenities? I hope she's not thinking of adding tennis courts and swimming pools. We might be able to work in a hot tub or sauna, but we're pretty much gridlocked with the road on two sides of the property and the neighbors on the other two sides."

Elle shook her head. "No, she's thinking of more adaptable, movable amenities. Although I know she's going to love the hot tub and sauna idea. So, prepare yourself for that. She wants to turn the Forsyth into an artists' retreat and eventually add a tearoom and spa. But those would come later."

Daniel hung on every word as Elle relayed what she, her mom and grandmother had talked about—possibly turning one or two of the outbuildings into a classroom or artist-in-residence space and converting an interior area into a studio for guests to set up easels to work. Perhaps they could even open the garden to local artists once a month or once a week as availability dictated—and possibly add a tearoom and spa at some point to offer guests a means to refresh and refill the creative well.

"That way we could stay true to the history of the inn with the traditional decor, but bring the place into the new millennium, as my mother would say."

"And you are staying around to help her implement the new plan?"

"I am. For a while. Until I have to go back to Atlanta."

His gut tightened at the thought of Elle being right here in Savannah.

"With your background in art, and knowing the area so well, you should consider being a permanent artist in residence."

"No," she said. "I've made a life for myself in Atlanta. I don't want to give that up."

He thought about asking her if she had someone special back in Atlanta but then decided he didn't want to know. A woman like Elle Clark probably didn't want for attention, even if she was spending the holidays here.

"We may even switch it up a bit and do art and architecture tours."

"That's a great idea," he said. "Before I started my business, I learned a lot about the architectural history of the city. If you need any help, let me know."

"Is that how you got interested in restoring local properties?"

He nodded. "When I left, I went to Orlando and I was so taken with the difference in the cities. I mean, Orlando is nice, and parts of the metro area like Winter Park are beautiful, but the city didn't have the same historical significance as Savannah. I missed it while I was gone. In fact, I couldn't wait to get back."

He started to add, *Even if a lot of people weren't very eager to welcome me back.* But he decided if he was going to move forward, he needed to leave the past in the past. He may have been a hooligan when he was a teenager, but he'd grown up, grown out of it. He'd changed. Didn't everyone deserve a chance to live down the stupidity of their youth?

That was something he needed to prove to Elle in actions, not deliver in lip service.

"I think we can make this happen."

Hell yeah. He'd make sure it happened.

Chapter Four

The next day, Elle sat at a table for two by the window in the riverfront restaurant The Rusty Gull, waiting for her grandmother. It was one of the best tables in the house because it overlooked the water. Even if the riverfront area was crowded with tourists, looking out at the serene water as she waited for Gigi to arrive gave Elle a moment to catch her breath.

It had been an odd morning. First, Gigi had insisted on having lunch, but then as Elle waited for her in the lobby, she'd found a note addressed to her from Gigi propped up near the guest book at the front desk. The note said that Kate had been able to work Gigi in for a hair appointment at the salon. Gigi said she was taking the appointment and would meet her at the restaurant at 1:30. The note was odd because Gigi had a standing weekly appointment with Kate for a wash and set. Kate always came to the inn after the salon closed to do Gigi's hair.

Maybe Kate was busy at their usual time this week? Maybe she had a date? Gigi would move mountains to accommodate her granddaughters if a date with a guy was involved.

Elle knew she would find out the rest of the story when Gigi arrived for lunch, but her grandmother was late.

Elle chuckled to herself. Gigi appreciated punctuality in others, but sometimes she lived by her own clock. More so now that she was eyeing retirement. Above everything, Elizabeth admired how she was still so active and independent at almost eighty-five.

She was feisty, that one.

In her younger years, before Gigi had taken over the inn from her own mother, she had trained as a chef. Everyone used to talk about how she had no trepidations about marching into a man's world and making her mark. She took such pride in the fact that Jane, her oldest granddaughter, had chosen to go to culinary school. Since Gigi had never fulfilled her own dream of opening a restaurant at the Forsyth, she was pinning her hopes on Jane to someday come home and make that unrequited dream come true. She'd loved Zelda's suggestion of building a tearoom. It had been the common ground they'd reached, which had eventually led to the meeting of the minds. Never mind that Jane was quite content in New York City. Zelda and Gigi had agreed they would work on Jane later.

Elle glanced at her watch—it was 1:38—and then

around the restaurant. Lacquered paneling in knotty pine served as a backdrop for old fishing nets hung with replicas of starfish, lobsters and crabs with a few Christmas ornaments tossed in. Santa hat wearing stuffed sailfish lined the upper walls nose to tail, like they were Rusty's answer to kitschy crown molding.

Why, out of all the places in Savannah, had Gigi chosen The Rusty Gull? As Elle scanned the place. She didn't see any familiar faces. Did Gigi want to talk about the remodel without the chance of running into curious neighbors or acquaintances? Not that anything they had to say about the remodel was particularly top secret.

Maybe Gigi wanted a change of pace. Occasionally, it was fun to don tourist hats and do as the visitors did.

The west wall housed a giant saltwater aquarium and the east was made of floor-to-ceiling windows that offered stunning views of the river. The place was tacky in that way touristy seafood restaurants tended to be. It wasn't exactly fine dining.

Not that she needed a fancy place, but this one looked like it hadn't been remodeled since they'd opened their doors back in 1972. She knew that date because the menu said so. It also promised good food—mostly fresh seafood caught locally—served in a rustic atmosphere.

Maybe she'd discover what she'd been missing out on all these years, having never given ol' Rusty a chance.

The server, whose name tag said Billie Jean, greeted her with a bowl of Rusty's famous blue-crab corn chowder before Elle had even had a chance to look over the menu.

Elle was about to tell her she hadn't ordered it, when

Billie Jean said, "Hey, hon. Your grandmother called and said she's running late. She wants you to start eating because she knows you're probably starving. You want me to bring you some sweet tea or something else to drink?"

Billie Jean was tall and thin, with curly black hair flecked with gray streaks. Her face looked weary, but her eyes were kind.

"Unsweet tea is fine, thanks," Elle said.

"Right away." She gave a little salute and turned her attention to a man who was signaling her from another table.

Turning her focus to the steaming bowl of chowder, Elle spooned up a bit and gazed out the window.

The sun was shining and sparkling off the water like diamonds. The river, with its sultry air and low-slung horizon, was one of the things she'd missed the most about Savannah. While Atlanta had every material thing a person could possibly want, it lacked the beauty and serenity of the low country.

When Daniel arrived at Rusty's, the place was still hopping with the lunch rush. He'd expected to wait, but when he gave the hostess his name, she'd said his table was ready. Maybe Wiladean was already there. She'd told him a quarter to two. He glanced at his watch to make sure he wasn't late. He still had three minutes to spare.

As Daniel followed the hostess, he locked gazes with a guy who was waiting for a table. The guy scowled and shook his head. Maybe the man thought he'd cut in line. He looked vaguely familiar and Daniel tried to place him.

"That guy over there—" Daniel tilted his head in the guy's direction "—maybe you should seat him first."

"Mr. Carlyle? Oh, no worries. I'll seat him and his party next."

Carlyle? George Carlyle. He'd owned the gas station where Daniel and his friends had driven off a couple of times without paying. That dirty look probably wasn't about the table.

Daniel had earned his bad reputation as a teenager. Even though the better part of a decade had gone by and he had a thriving business that focused on bettering the community, occasionally he ran into someone who still thought of him as the shady kid who caused trouble and whose only interests were stealing gas, procuring illegal fireworks and burning down houses.

As he passed, he nodded to Carlyle, who deepened his scowl.

No regrets and only new mistakes: that was the code he lived by now.

Despite encountering the occasional old-timer with a good long-term memory, he knew most people had forgiven the past and accepted who he was today. After his grandmother's house had burned down, he'd been in a hurry to get the hell out of Savannah—He figured his grandma and Aidan would be better off without him. He'd moved to Orlando and worked two, sometimes three jobs at a time doing construction and whatever work he could find to support himself and send money to his grandmother. It was the least he could do after the trouble he'd caused.

A flash of long blond hair caught his eye.

He saw Elle before she saw him. She was seated at a table for two next to the window facing him, but gazing out at the water. A bowl of soup was in front of her, a spoon poised in her hand. She wore a skirt and blouse, a sweater and heels. Her legs were crossed at the ankles and angled to the side so that his gaze trailed down and lit on strong, long, tanned legs and worked its way up to full breasts showcased nicely by the sweater.

He forced his gaze to her face before she caught him looking. But hell, he'd have to be a dead man to not appreciate what he saw.

As the hostess led him to her table, her gaze found his.

She looked a little startled but managed to return a polite, if somewhat stiff, smile as she set down her spoon.

"Here you go, this is your table," the hostess said.

"What are you doing here, Daniel?"

"I was supposed to meet Wiladean here to discuss the renovation."

"Really? Gigi is meeting me here, too. She's finishing up with a hair appointment. But she'll be here any minute…um…okay…huh… She didn't mention you were coming to lunch, too."

"Hey there, honey." The server, Billie Jean, smiled at him and set a bowl of soup in front of him. "What can I get ya to drink?"

"I didn't order soup. We're waiting for someone. I'll just have some tea for now."

"Well, if you're waiting for Wiladean, she called

again and she can't make it. Looks like it will just be you two."

Elle's mouth fell open and her expression suggested she smelled something fishy, and it wasn't the fresh catch of the day.

"She said she's real sorry, but y'all should go ahead and have lunch without her. It's her treat." Billie Jean sighed. "Y'all make a real cute couple."

Elizabeth's cheeks flushed, and Daniel couldn't remember the last time he'd seen a woman blush like that.

"A couple? Us?" Elle laughed. "No. No way. We are not a couple."

Daniel wondered if she realized this was the second time in as many days that someone had mentioned how good they looked together. He could see it.

"I'm not dating anyone right now," Elle said. "You see, I was engaged a few years ago. But I got stood up at the altar."

Billie Jean's lips formed an O shape and she placed a hand on Elle's arm. "Oh, honey, I'm so sorry. I can see how that would put you off dating."

Elle slanted a glance at Daniel before looking back at Billie Jean. "Yes, it was pretty horrific. You see, my ex-fiancé's best man talked him out of getting married. Can you believe that?"

Billie Jean's mouth fell open and her eyes flashed, greedy for the gossip. "Get out. Are you kidding me? The best man? What kind of a lousy jerk would do a thing like that?"

"I know. Right?" Elle's gaze bore into Daniel. "But wait, it gets better. Right before I was supposed to walk down the aisle, my sister heard my ex-fiancé and his so-called friend talking. She heard the best man tell him to get out while he could. My sister wasn't sure if she should tell me. But when the ceremony started and she saw my fiancé standing at the altar, naturally, she assumed everything was fine. That my fiancé was better than that. But *no*. Right after the minister asked him if he took me to be his wife, he couldn't answer. His best man leaned in and nudged him. I thought he was trying to help, but then, he tells Roger—that's my ex's name—'Don't do this. Leave. Now.' And Roger ran out of the church like he was being chased. He left me standing there. Humiliated in front of more than two hundred fifty people. I don't think I'll ever be able to forgive either one of them."

"Honey, I don't blame you one bit," Billie Jean said. "Both of 'em deserve to rot in hell. I'm so sorry that happened to you. Maybe y'all would like a glass of wine rather than tea? It's on the house if ya do. You deserve it after all you went through."

"That's sweet of you," Elle said. "But tea is fine."

Billie Jean looked at Daniel. "If she's having lunch with you after going through all that, you must be a pretty good guy. There aren't enough good guys in the world. And honey—" she leaned in to Elle "—this one is *cu-u-te*. Maybe you should rethink sending him to the friend zone. I'll be right back with your drinks."

Okay. So, Elle was making a point. He got it. Loud and clear. She was still angry. Obviously, Elle didn't know the whole story or she wouldn't be *this* mad at *him*. Hurt? Sure, he could understand that, but grudge-holding-furious for years? No, she didn't know the half of what had happened that day.

"Do you feel better now?" Daniel asked.

"I don't know who I'm more angry with," said Elle. "You or Gigi. I've already told her to stop trying to push us together."

He narrowed his eyes. "Is that what she's trying to do?"

Elle looked down at her hands for a few beats before raising her chin and looking at him like he was an idiot. But she hadn't gotten up and walked out.

"Why else would she set up a lunch with us and not show?"

Daniel couldn't help it, he laughed.

"Your grandmother has a lot of great qualities, but subtlety isn't a strength."

"It never has been," Elle said.

His gut was telling him to tread carefully. As tempting as she might be, this was not a date. Even though Wiladean was the instigator, Elle was her granddaughter, and if things went south with Elle, it might upset Wiladean and he might lose the job. Sure, he had enough work, but Wiladean was an opinion maker. Just as she'd helped give his business some clout over the years, she was connected enough to take back all that goodwill.

"Look, we're here," he said. "We might as well talk about the renovation. As your grandmother said, you're the voice of reason in this project. It's probably a good time for you to tell me everything I need to know."

Before Elle could answer, Billie Jean approached with their tea.

"Wiladean wants the two of you to enjoy lunch without her. She said to tell you it's her treat. And that y'all should get anything you want, including dessert."

Billie Jean's eyes flashed bright as if she'd received the news that she'd won the lottery. In a way, she had. No doubt, Wiladean had tipped Billie Jean well to enlist her help in pulling off this crazy scheme.

"Take your time. Talk and get acquainted. I'll come back to get your order."

As soon as Billie Jean walked away, Elle said, "I'm sorry she's put us on the spot like this. You don't have to stay."

"And miss out on this soup? Are you kidding? I mean, if you want to leave, please." He gestured toward the door, silently willing her to stay.

"No, I'm staying. Because soup *and* lunch is on Gigi. We need to take full advantage of that to teach her a lesson. In fact, maybe we should order a couple of seafood towers."

"I'm paying for lunch," Daniel said.

When Elle started to protest, he held up his hand. "That's nonnegotiable."

"You don't have to do that," she said.

"Why not?"

"Because Gigi stood us up—because she was conniving and trying to set us up. And I'll feel bad."

"Why should you feel bad? You weren't the one who planned the bait and switch. Or were you in on it?"

He loved the way her eyes flashed.

"Absolutely not." She scooted her chair back and stood up in one swift motion. "Look, this is awkward. I apologize on my grandmother's behalf. I'm going to go."

"Elle, don't leave."

She frowned at him and shook her head as she hitched her purse up on her shoulder.

"You always did run when things got tough," Daniel said.

"No, I don't. You're the one who left town."

She stopped, crossed her arms and caught her bottom lip between her front teeth.

"So did you," Daniel said. "Look, don't go. Please."

Elizabeth hesitated a moment. Then she sat down at the table again.

"Thank you," he said.

Her eyes flashed again. "For what?"

"For staying."

Her brows were knitted and he could see the pain in her eyes. She sighed loudly, and for a moment he was afraid she was going to stand up again.

"Can we talk about this?"

"About what, Daniel?"

"About you and me—"

"There is no you and me."

"I know there's no *you and me*. What I was trying to ask was can we talk about what happened between you and me—at the church that day. I know you think you have a reason to dislike me. If you need someone to blame, it's okay if you don't want to talk and you want to spend the rest of your life blaming me. I'll never bring it up again. But if you want to know the rest of the story—because you only know one side—we can talk about it."

She stared at him for a moment, as if letting his words sink in. As if maybe the words were even sinking in and settling in against her will.

"Daniel, I don't want to do this here."

"Okay." He signaled to the server. "Let's pay the

check and get out of here. Let's go somewhere else and talk."

"No, I don't want to talk about it." The words were there, but the edge was blunted.

Billie Jean stepped up to their table. "Are y'all ready to order?"

"No, just the check, please, Billie Jean," Daniel said.

"Separate checks," Elizabeth said.

"But y'all haven't even had your lunch yet. You only had the soup—and you didn't finish it. Is everything okay?"

"The soup was delicious," he said. "We have to go. An unexpected meeting came up."

Billie Jean raised a brow. "An unexpected meeting, huh?" She looked at Elle and then back at Daniel. "Is that what you kids are calling it these days? Well, you're in luck the bill has been paid. Your grandma took care of it. You're free to go."

As Billie Jean walked away, Daniel's phone rang. Normally he wouldn't have answered it, but the words *Savannah-Chatham Metropolitan Police* appeared on the caller ID. "This is weird. It says it's the police. I'm sorry, but I'd better take it."

Elle nodded and they both started walking toward the exit.

"This is Daniel Quindlin," he said as they walked.

"Daniel Quindlin, this is Sergeant Eric Briggs of the Savannah-Chatham Metropolitan Police Department. Are you related to an Aidan Quindlin?"

As his blood ran cold in anticipation of what the sergeant was about to say, Daniel put his free hand over his ear to block out the background noise of convivial chatter, clattering silverware and crying babies.

"Aidan is my brother." Daniel's mouth went dry and his voice seemed disassociated with his body. "Is everything okay?"

"What's wrong?" Elle whispered. All animosity that had previously darkened her voice was replaced by genuine concern. He realized he was no longer walking and had frozen in place.

"Sir, are you in the Savannah area?"

"I am. Why?" This time his words were a little more forceful. "Tell me what's wrong."

"Can you please come to Memorial University Hospital as soon as possible?"

"Yeah. Sure. Is Aidan okay? Is he hurt?"

"Sir, please come to the hospital and they can give you more information."

The sergeant ended the call.

Daniel stood there for a moment, trying to get his bearings.

"Daniel, is everything okay? What's wrong?"

Elle's hand was on his arm. The brows above her blue eyes were furrowed in concern.

She was a touchstone that snapped him back to reality.

"I don't know. That was the Savannah Police. They asked me about Aidan. My brother. They told me to come to Memorial University Hospital."

Elle's hand fluttered to her mouth. "Oh, my God. I hope he's okay."

Daniel shook his head a little harder than necessary, trying to shake away the fog.

"I do, too, but I don't know. They wouldn't tell me."

"Come on," Elle said. "I'm going to drive you."

ve to call the school and tell them about Aidan's
t. But I don't know the number and I can't—"
ere does she go to school and what's her name?"
e goes to Country Day. I'll have to talk to them."
look up the number for you," Elle said. "Sit
" Her voice was gentle but firm. He did what she
owering himself onto the vinyl seat again.
you remember Josey Jensen?" she asked. "We
o school with her."
niel gave a dazed, noncommittal shrug.
ne's the dean of students at Country Day now,"
lle. "Do you want me to talk to her and explain
happened?"
o," Daniel said. "Let me call the school."
le nodded. After she pulled up the number, she
t to him. He punched it into his phone and then
ed away, toward the hall that led to the exit.
few minutes later, he returned looking a little
ish.
hloe gets out of school in about an hour. Is there
vay you'd be able to go get her? I would, but I don't
to leave the hospital in case the doctor finishes
n's surgery. I want to be here."
Of course," Elle said, happy she could be useful.
t the end of the school day, your friend Josey is
g to get Chloe from her class and bring her to the
e. She said it's fine if you pick her up."
How about if I take her to the inn?" Elle suggested.
m and Gigi will take good care of her. That way
come back and bring you something to eat. We
did get to eat lunch. You must be starving."
was a dumb thing to say. She knew it as soon as

Chapter Five

Elle remembered Aidan Quindlin, even though she
didn't know him very well. When he and his grandmother had moved into the inn after the fire, he mostly
kept to himself. He was a couple of years younger than
Daniel. He'd run in a different circle at Savannah Country Day. Aidan had dated her sister Kate. Elle seemed to
remember some kind of drama surrounding their prom.
Even so, that didn't matter now. She was here to help
Daniel. He seemed shocked and scared and human as
he'd gotten official word that his brother had been in a
motorcycle accident.

A day drinker ran a red light.
The helmet saved his life.
Still...head trauma. Possible spinal cord injuries.
Suddenly all her past differences with Daniel melted

away, or at least faded into the background. Any decent person would help in Aidan's time of need. Their grandmother and parents were gone. The fact that Daniel had gotten the call and he was Aidan's only next of kin in the hospital waiting room answered the question Elle couldn't ask—about whether Aidan was married or had someone special in his life. It appeared that the Quindlin brothers only had each other.

The waiting room was decorated for the holidays. Someone had decorated the windows with canned spray snow and stencils. A small artificial tree sat atop one of the end tables and an instrumental version of "The Christmas Song" played softly through the overhead speakers. She watched Daniel, who was sitting forward on the gray-green vinyl waiting room chair with his elbows on his knees, hands clasped and head down.

They'd been sitting in silence for about an hour.

"Do you want something to drink?" she asked him. "I'll go get us something."

Daniel lifted his head and blinked at her as if he'd just remembered she was there.

"No. Thanks." He rubbed his hands over his face, raking them back through his curly dark brown hair before returning his elbows to their resting spot on his knees. "Uh…you don't need to stay. I don't want to hold you up."

"Don't be ridiculous. I'm not going to leave you alone at the hospital. Besides, I drove you here. How would you get home?"

He studied his clasped hands. Then looked back at her. Pain was etched into his handsome face, though she

could tell he was trying to act li[...] erything. "I can Uber it. Don't wo[...]

Elle stood. "No, I'm not going [...] I won't. But I will go get us som[...] take yours?"

He watched her for a few beats [...] unreadable. She could've talked h[...] that he looked relieved. Finally, he [...]

She nodded. "I'll be right back [...] go on her errand, she thought ab[...] cell number and telling him to ca[...] news, but then she thought better [...] was only going to the hospital cafet[...] be gone long.

Still, life could change on a dime [...] were in a tourist trap restaurant obses[...] ferences, and the next, someone you [...] ing to life.

And she hadn't cleared the waitin[...] heard him utter an expletive. When s[...] on his feet, looking at his watch.

"What's wrong?" Elle asked, retu[...]

"Chloe," he murmured. "My br[...] She's in school. Aidan usually picks [...] time. I have to call the school."

Aidan had a daughter? Where w[...] mother? Obviously, this wasn't the ti[...] she wasn't here at the hospital and Da[...] ing on her to pick up the child.

He fumbled with his cell phone [...] with the slow internet.

"Daniel, let me help," she said. "[...]

the words passed her lips. Food was probably the last thing on his mind... Then again, he was a guy. Not to stereotype, but most guys could usually eat whenever and whatever food appeared in front of them. And Daniel wasn't balking at the suggestion.

"Daniel, she's going to wonder why a total stranger is picking her up from school. What would you like me to tell her?"

Daniel shrugged and a muscle in his jaw twitched. "She's five years old. What do you tell a five-year-old in a case like this?"

"I'm a teacher. Unless you have something specific you want me to tell her, you can leave it to me. I'll handle it. But I do need your cell number just in case."

As he rattled off the numbers, she punched them into her phone and then called him.

"Now you have my number, too. Just in case."

He nodded as he silenced his phone.

"I'm going to go get Chloe now—"

"Elle, I remembered something. Chloe won't get into a car with anyone unless the person knows the special code word she and Aidan came up with."

"Oh, good. That's important. Do you know it?"

Daniel smiled sadly. "Yeah. It's rutabaga. The word makes Chloe laugh."

Elle held his gaze and smiled. "I'll bet it sounds funny to a five-year-old. Don't worry about anything. I'll take good care of Chloe."

"Wait," Daniel said. "You're going to need a car seat. There's one in Aidan's car. He takes Chloe to school in the car and rides his bike around town until he picks her up."

Aidan didn't strike her as the type who'd ride a motorcycle. A scooter, maybe, but not a bike. She didn't mean to judge, but from what she remembered, he'd been somewhat of a nerd. It was hard to reconcile that Aidan with the one who'd been in the motorcycle accident.

People probably remembered her as the nerdy Clark sister. Jane was the beauty, and Kate was the cool sister.

Elle had been the bookish good girl, who had fought her attraction to the bad boy.

Possibly similar to the way Aidan had been drawn to Kate.

Maybe Aidan had been a late bloomer? Because now he had a kid. And a motorcycle.

Sadness pulled at Elle's insides.

"I wonder if the school has some on hand for emergencies?" Elle suggested.

"That's a good idea."

Daniel placed the call and a few minutes later, they had secured a loaner from the school.

"Call me if anything changes," Elle said as she prepared to leave.

His brows knitted and he frowned. He didn't say it, but she could virtually read his mind. *What good would that do? You'll be there. I'll be here. I'll handle it.*

"See you soon." She walked away so that he didn't have to answer.

Daniel and Aidan had started getting their act together this year when they'd decided to go into business together.

An architect, Aidan was the brains behind Quindlin Brothers Renovations. Daniel was the brawn.

Growing up, they'd never been particularly close because they had always been too different. When their parents died in the car accident, it had only magnified their differences. Daniel was the rebel who hadn't wanted to move to Savannah in his senior year of high school to live with their grandmother and he'd done everything to prove exactly how deep his discontent ran. He'd been so self-absorbed he hadn't had time to worry about his younger brother, who'd tried hard to make up for all of Daniel's shortcomings by being the perfect kid.

Aidan had been the smart one, the studious one. The one who never caused anyone a lick of grief. The anomaly was that damn motorcycle. Even when he was trying to be a bad ass, he'd worn a helmet. If he hadn't, he'd be dead right now. But a straitlaced guy like Aidan should've never been on a hog like that in the first place.

After Veronica walked out on him and Chloe, Aidan seemed like he had something to prove. That was when he'd bought the bike.

Daniel stared past his calloused hands, past the work-tanned skin of his arms to the dingy linoleum of the waiting room floor. Why hadn't he taken a stronger stand when Aidan bought the Harley? First, because Aidan was an adult. Daniel couldn't tell him what to do. Second, the bike had been an impulse purchase.

Even so, he'd even gone to motorcycle school to learn how to ride the thing. But nothing could prepare a person for two tons of steel powered by a drunk blowing through a red light. Just like nothing Daniel could've said would've changed Aidan's mind about keeping the bike. As much as Daniel wanted to believe he had that kind of power over his kid brother, he didn't.

Daniel may have been the street-smart Quindlin brother, but Aidan was supposed to be the one with the most common sense.

He uttered a swear word under his breath, cursing his brother for not using his brain when it mattered.

His legs began to tingle and he realized he'd been sitting hunched over, staring at the floor for a long time. He stood and glanced at his watch. Elle should've made it to the school by now. He wondered what she'd say to Chloe. He hadn't been any more help to Elle when she'd asked for his guidance on what to say than he'd been about setting his brother straight on how dumb it was to buy a bike when he had a five-year-old who depended on him.

It wouldn't do anyone any good for him to sit around grousing. He needed to borrow a page from Elle and think about the bigger picture rather than being pissed off at his brother for almost killing himself.

Despite Elle's personal beef with him, she'd turned it off and focused on what really mattered in the face of a crisis. Here she was coming to his rescue again, like she had the night he'd accidentally burned down his grandmother's house. She'd been the one to tell her mom and grandmother about the fire and Wiladean Boudreau and Zelda Clark had welcomed his grandmother and Aidan, refusing to accept a penny after all was said and done.

Wiladean and Zelda didn't know it, but Daniel intended to repay their kindness by doing their reno at cost. Or at least that had been his intention, until Aidan's accident.

Now everything was on hold until he knew Aidan's prognosis.

He paced the length of the empty waiting room a few times, trying to burn off some of his anxious steam, but it wasn't helping.

"Aw, hell."

He decided to check in with Elle and ask how Chloe was doing.

He had started typing the text when someone said, "Mr. Quindlin?"

Daniel looked up to see a guy wearing surgical scrubs and a grim expression.

Ah, the resiliency of a well-adjusted child.

Elle couldn't decide if it was heartening or frightening how willingly and happily Chloe Quindlin went with her. All it took was the utterance of the secret word and a promise of ice cream and the Disney Channel and she was in the back seat, strapped into a car seat the school had loaned Elle.

"We had a party at school today." Chloe's little voice drifted from the back seat. "'Cause today is the last day of school for the rest of the year."

Elle glanced in the rearview mirror and saw the little girl in the booster seat, gazing out the side window.

"Are you on vacation now, Chloe?"

"Yes."

Elle stole another glance in the rearview mirror and saw her clutching a white stuffed kitten, cooing softly to it.

Her curly brown hair and big blue eyes made her look like a porcelain doll.

"What's your kitty's name?" Elle asked.

"Princess Sweetie Pie." The little girl held the stuffed animal up to her ear. "Princess Sweetie Pie wants to know where we are going."

"Tell Princess Sweetie Pie we are going to my house. In fact, we are almost there. Your Uncle Daniel is going to pick you up a little bit later. But while we're waiting for him, we can get something to eat and play games. Do you like to play games?"

"It depends on what game it is."

They kept a good assortment of games and puzzles at the inn for various age groups.

"Have you ever played the game Candyland?"

"No."

Elle stopped at a red light at Whitaker and Gaston. In the rearview mirror, she saw the little girl hold her cat up to her ear again. "Princess Sweetie Pie wants to know if you have the game My Little Pony? That's her favorite."

The light turned green and Elle looked both ways before she accelerated through the intersection. "I'm not sure. We can look when we get inside."

She made a right turn onto Hall Street and parked in one of the reserved spots.

"This house is big. Is it your house?"

"It sure is. Want to come inside?"

The little girl hugged Princess Sweetie Pie but didn't answer the question. Elle got out of the car and opened the back door. As she unbuckled Chloe from her booster

Chapter Five

Elle remembered Aidan Quindlin, even though she didn't know him very well. When he and his grandmother had moved into the inn after the fire, he mostly kept to himself. He was a couple of years younger than Daniel. He'd run in a different circle at Savannah Country Day. Aidan had dated her sister Kate. Elle seemed to remember some kind of drama surrounding their prom. Even so, that didn't matter now. She was here to help Daniel. He seemed shocked and scared and human as he'd gotten official word that his brother had been in a motorcycle accident.

A day drinker ran a red light.

The helmet saved his life.

Still...head trauma. Possible spinal cord injuries.

Suddenly all her past differences with Daniel melted

away, or at least faded into the background. Any decent person would help in Aidan's time of need. Their grandmother and parents were gone. The fact that Daniel had gotten the call and he was Aidan's only next of kin in the hospital waiting room answered the question Elle couldn't ask—about whether Aidan was married or had someone special in his life. It appeared that the Quindlin brothers only had each other.

The waiting room was decorated for the holidays. Someone had decorated the windows with canned spray snow and stencils. A small artificial tree sat atop one of the end tables and an instrumental version of "The Christmas Song" played softly through the overhead speakers. She watched Daniel, who was sitting forward on the gray-green vinyl waiting room chair with his elbows on his knees, hands clasped and head down.

They'd been sitting in silence for about an hour.

"Do you want something to drink?" she asked him. "I'll go get us something."

Daniel lifted his head and blinked at her as if he'd just remembered she was there.

"No. Thanks." He rubbed his hands over his face, raking them back through his curly dark brown hair before returning his elbows to their resting spot on his knees. "Uh…you don't need to stay. I don't want to hold you up."

"Don't be ridiculous. I'm not going to leave you alone at the hospital. Besides, I drove you here. How would you get home?"

He studied his clasped hands. Then looked back at her. Pain was etched into his handsome face, though she could tell he was trying to act like he was handling everything. "I can Uber it. Don't worry about me. Just go."

Elle stood. "No, I'm not going to *just go*. Sorry, but I won't. But I will go get us some coffee. How do you take yours?"

He watched her for a few beats. His expression was unreadable. She could've talked herself into believing that he looked relieved. Finally, he said, "Black."

She nodded. "I'll be right back." As she turned to go on her errand, she thought about rattling off her cell number and telling him to call her if he got any news, but then she thought better of it. Besides, she was only going to the hospital cafeteria. She wouldn't be gone long.

Still, life could change on a dime. One minute you were in a tourist trap restaurant obsessing over past differences, and the next, someone you loved was clinging to life.

And she hadn't cleared the waiting room when she heard him utter an expletive. When she turned, he was on his feet, looking at his watch.

"What's wrong?" Elle asked, returning to his side.

"Chloe," he murmured. "My brother's daughter. She's in school. Aidan usually picks her up around this time. I have to call the school."

Aidan had a daughter? Where was the little girl's mother? Obviously, this wasn't the time to ask, because she wasn't here at the hospital and Daniel wasn't counting on her to pick up the child.

He fumbled with his cell phone and got frustrated with the slow internet.

"Daniel, let me help," she said. "Please."

"I have to call the school and tell them about Aidan's accident. But I don't know the number and I can't—"

"Where does she go to school and what's her name?"

"She goes to Country Day. I'll have to talk to them."

"I'll look up the number for you," Elle said. "Sit down." Her voice was gentle but firm. He did what she said, lowering himself onto the vinyl seat again.

"Do you remember Josey Jensen?" she asked. "We went to school with her."

Daniel gave a dazed, noncommittal shrug.

"She's the dean of students at Country Day now," said Elle. "Do you want me to talk to her and explain what happened?"

"No," Daniel said. "Let me call the school."

Elle nodded. After she pulled up the number, she read it to him. He punched it into his phone and then walked away, toward the hall that led to the exit.

A few minutes later, he returned looking a little sheepish.

"Chloe gets out of school in about an hour. Is there any way you'd be able to go get her? I would, but I don't want to leave the hospital in case the doctor finishes Aidan's surgery. I want to be here."

"Of course," Elle said, happy she could be useful.

"At the end of the school day, your friend Josey is going to get Chloe from her class and bring her to the office. She said it's fine if you pick her up."

"How about if I take her to the inn?" Elle suggested. "Mom and Gigi will take good care of her. That way I can come back and bring you something to eat. We never did get to eat lunch. You must be starving."

It was a dumb thing to say. She knew it as soon as

the words passed her lips. Food was probably the last thing on his mind… Then again, he was a guy. Not to stereotype, but most guys could usually eat whenever and whatever food appeared in front of them. And Daniel wasn't balking at the suggestion.

"Daniel, she's going to wonder why a total stranger is picking her up from school. What would you like me to tell her?"

Daniel shrugged and a muscle in his jaw twitched. "She's five years old. What do you tell a five-year-old in a case like this?"

"I'm a teacher. Unless you have something specific you want me to tell her, you can leave it to me. I'll handle it. But I do need your cell number just in case."

As he rattled off the numbers, she punched them into her phone and then called him.

"Now you have my number, too. Just in case."

He nodded as he silenced his phone.

"I'm going to go get Chloe now—"

"Elle, I remembered something. Chloe won't get into a car with anyone unless the person knows the special code word she and Aidan came up with."

"Oh, good. That's important. Do you know it?"

Daniel smiled sadly. "Yeah. It's rutabaga. The word makes Chloe laugh."

Elle held his gaze and smiled. "I'll bet it sounds funny to a five-year-old. Don't worry about anything. I'll take good care of Chloe."

"Wait," Daniel said. "You're going to need a car seat. There's one in Aidan's car. He takes Chloe to school in the car and rides his bike around town until he picks her up."

Aidan didn't strike her as the type who'd ride a motorcycle. A scooter, maybe, but not a bike. She didn't mean to judge, but from what she remembered, he'd been somewhat of a nerd. It was hard to reconcile that Aidan with the one who'd been in the motorcycle accident.

People probably remembered her as the nerdy Clark sister. Jane was the beauty, and Kate was the cool sister.

Elle had been the bookish good girl, who had fought her attraction to the bad boy.

Possibly similar to the way Aidan had been drawn to Kate.

Maybe Aidan had been a late bloomer? Because now he had a kid. And a motorcycle.

Sadness pulled at Elle's insides.

"I wonder if the school has some on hand for emergencies?" Elle suggested.

"That's a good idea."

Daniel placed the call and a few minutes later, they had secured a loaner from the school.

"Call me if anything changes," Elle said as she prepared to leave.

His brows knitted and he frowned. He didn't say it, but she could virtually read his mind. *What good would that do? You'll be there. I'll be here. I'll handle it.*

"See you soon." She walked away so that he didn't have to answer.

Daniel and Aidan had started getting their act together this year when they'd decided to go into business together.

An architect, Aidan was the brains behind Quindlin Brothers Renovations. Daniel was the brawn.

Growing up, they'd never been particularly close because they had always been too different. When their parents died in the car accident, it had only magnified their differences. Daniel was the rebel who hadn't wanted to move to Savannah in his senior year of high school to live with their grandmother and he'd done everything to prove exactly how deep his discontent ran. He'd been so self-absorbed he hadn't had time to worry about his younger brother, who'd tried hard to make up for all of Daniel's shortcomings by being the perfect kid.

Aidan had been the smart one, the studious one. The one who never caused anyone a lick of grief. The anomaly was that damn motorcycle. Even when he was trying to be a bad ass, he'd worn a helmet. If he hadn't, he'd be dead right now. But a straitlaced guy like Aidan should've never been on a hog like that in the first place.

After Veronica walked out on him and Chloe, Aidan seemed like he had something to prove. That was when he'd bought the bike.

Daniel stared past his calloused hands, past the work-tanned skin of his arms to the dingy linoleum of the waiting room floor. Why hadn't he taken a stronger stand when Aidan bought the Harley? First, because Aidan was an adult. Daniel couldn't tell him what to do. Second, the bike had been an impulse purchase.

Even so, he'd even gone to motorcycle school to learn how to ride the thing. But nothing could prepare a person for two tons of steel powered by a drunk blowing through a red light. Just like nothing Daniel could've said would've changed Aidan's mind about keeping the bike. As much as Daniel wanted to believe he had that kind of power over his kid brother, he didn't.

Daniel may have been the street-smart Quindlin brother, but Aidan was supposed to be the one with the most common sense.

He uttered a swear word under his breath, cursing his brother for not using his brain when it mattered.

His legs began to tingle and he realized he'd been sitting hunched over, staring at the floor for a long time. He stood and glanced at his watch. Elle should've made it to the school by now. He wondered what she'd say to Chloe. He hadn't been any more help to Elle when she'd asked for his guidance on what to say than he'd been about setting his brother straight on how dumb it was to buy a bike when he had a five-year-old who depended on him.

It wouldn't do anyone any good for him to sit around grousing. He needed to borrow a page from Elle and think about the bigger picture rather than being pissed off at his brother for almost killing himself.

Despite Elle's personal beef with him, she'd turned it off and focused on what really mattered in the face of a crisis. Here she was coming to his rescue again, like she had the night he'd accidentally burned down his grandmother's house. She'd been the one to tell her mom and grandmother about the fire and Wiladean Boudreau and Zelda Clark had welcomed his grandmother and Aidan, refusing to accept a penny after all was said and done.

Wiladean and Zelda didn't know it, but Daniel intended to repay their kindness by doing their reno at cost. Or at least that had been his intention, until Aidan's accident.

Now everything was on hold until he knew Aidan's prognosis.

He paced the length of the empty waiting room a few times, trying to burn off some of his anxious steam, but it wasn't helping.

"Aw, hell."

He decided to check in with Elle and ask how Chloe was doing.

He had started typing the text when someone said, "Mr. Quindlin?"

Daniel looked up to see a guy wearing surgical scrubs and a grim expression.

Ah, the resiliency of a well-adjusted child.

Elle couldn't decide if it was heartening or frightening how willingly and happily Chloe Quindlin went with her. All it took was the utterance of the secret word and a promise of ice cream and the Disney Channel and she was in the back seat, strapped into a car seat the school had loaned Elle.

"We had a party at school today." Chloe's little voice drifted from the back seat. "'Cause today is the last day of school for the rest of the year."

Elle glanced in the rearview mirror and saw the little girl in the booster seat, gazing out the side window.

"Are you on vacation now, Chloe?"

"Yes."

Elle stole another glance in the rearview mirror and saw her clutching a white stuffed kitten, cooing softly to it.

Her curly brown hair and big blue eyes made her look like a porcelain doll.

"What's your kitty's name?" Elle asked.

"Princess Sweetie Pie." The little girl held the stuffed animal up to her ear. "Princess Sweetie Pie wants to know where we are going."

"Tell Princess Sweetie Pie we are going to my house. In fact, we are almost there. Your Uncle Daniel is going to pick you up a little bit later. But while we're waiting for him, we can get something to eat and play games. Do you like to play games?"

"It depends on what game it is."

They kept a good assortment of games and puzzles at the inn for various age groups.

"Have you ever played the game Candyland?"

"No."

Elle stopped at a red light at Whitaker and Gaston. In the rearview mirror, she saw the little girl hold her cat up to her ear again. "Princess Sweetie Pie wants to know if you have the game My Little Pony? That's her favorite."

The light turned green and Elle looked both ways before she accelerated through the intersection. "I'm not sure. We can look when we get inside."

She made a right turn onto Hall Street and parked in one of the reserved spots.

"This house is big. Is it your house?"

"It sure is. Want to come inside?"

The little girl hugged Princess Sweetie Pie but didn't answer the question. Elle got out of the car and opened the back door. As she unbuckled Chloe from her booster seat, the little girl asked, "Why are you picking me up from school? My daddy always picks me up."

Elle knew the question was coming and she supposed she should have been grateful that Chloe waited to ask until they were off the road.

"I'm glad you asked me that question, Chloe," Elle said. "You know the only reason it was okay for you to go in the car with me was because I knew the code word. Ms. Jensen talked to your Uncle Daniel. He's the one who sent me to get you and he'll be here to pick you up later. I'm glad you know it's not okay to leave with anyone you don't know unless they know the code or another adult you know says it's okay."

The little girl's eyes got big and her bottom lip protruded. Elle feared she might have scared her with all the "stranger danger" talk. Maybe she was saying too much.

In her experience of dealing with her students, she'd learned to only answer the questions they asked. Not to elaborate or add too much. Since Daniel hadn't been able to give her any guidance on what to tell Chloe about her father, she knew the only thing she could do was tell the truth. But maybe the less she said the better, since Elle didn't know much about Aidan's condition. Although Chloe seemed like a smart, well-adjusted child, she was a little girl.

"Honey, your daddy had to go see the doctor. Have you ever been to the doctor, Chloe?"

The little girl nodded and plucked her white cat out from under her arm and held it up to her ear. Then she held it in front of her face and spoke to it. "I'll ask her.

Princess Sweetie Pie wants to know if Daddy has to get a shot."

"He might."

Chloe winced. "Poor daddy."

"I know," Elle said. "Nobody likes to get shots. But you know what I do like?"

Chloe shook her head and looked at her expectantly.

"I like ice cream. Do you?"

Her curls bobbed as she nodded. "So does Princess Sweetie Pie."

"I'm sure we have enough for three. Want to go in and get some?"

Elle lifted Chloe and Princess Sweetie Pie from the car seat and set them down on the gravel walkway. She took the little girl's hand and led her to the back door. They walked straight into the kitchen.

Gigi was in there waiting for them. Elle had called to let her mom and Gigi know about the accident. This wasn't how she'd thought the day would go. She had fully intended to come home and give Gigi a firm talking to about skipping out on the luncheon meeting with Daniel Quindlin and tell her—again—that she needed to stop trying to push them together. But suddenly, being there with Daniel when the call came seemed like divine intervention. If not for the attempted lunchtime fix-up, she wouldn't have been there to pick up Chloe and to help Daniel and Aidan.

Who would've thought she'd ever hear herself say that? But suddenly everything that had gone on before seemed unimportant right now.

"You must be Chloe," Gigi said, squatting down in

front of the little girl as best as her knees would allow her to do. "You can call me Gigi."

Chloe looked small and unsure, standing stoically in the middle of the kitchen, hugging her white cat.

Even though Elle had planned on giving her grandmother a pass…for the most part…it didn't mean she couldn't let her know that she was wise to her matchmaking plan.

"Your hair looks pretty, Gigi," Elle said, as she took two containers of ice cream out of the freezer. Even though Gigi took pride in looking her best, it was perfectly clear that she hadn't had a thing done to her hair today.

"Well, thank you, honey."

"It was awfully nice of Kate to work you in on the spur of the moment like that. Is that a new style?"

Elle smiled a knowing smile and arched a brow at her to drive home her point.

Gigi didn't even have the good grace to look sheepish. Instead, she stood up and patted her hair. "Yes, your sister does such a good job, and she's so good to her Gigi."

The part Gigi didn't say, but mentally telegraphed to Elle was, *You should follow Kate's example.*

Now wasn't the time to hash it out. Gigi must have realized it, too, because she changed the subject.

She walked over to Elle and took one of the halfgallon containers out of her hands. "How are things?" she asked, cautiously lowering her voice.

Elle was certain her grandmother wasn't asking about the lunch. "I'm not sure," Elle answered. "I was going to text Daniel after I got Chloe the ice cream I promised her. Would you like to join us for ice cream, Gigi?" she said a little louder, infusing the invitation with the tried-and-true enthusiasm of an elementary school teacher for Chloe's benefit.

Gigi answered with an exaggerated smile that she directed to Chloe. "I'd love to. Chloe? May I join you? I'd love some ice cream. In fact, we might as well splurge and go all out. Chloe, what would you think about making ice cream sundaes?" Chloe looked confused. "You know, ice cream with chocolate sauce and sprinkles and whipped cream. And I'll bet if Elle looks in the fridge, she'll find a brand-new jar of maraschino cherries."

Chloe brightened up a little bit. "I like cherries and sprinkles on my ice cream."

"Well, then that's what we will have," Gigi said. "You go on over there and you and your cat get yourselves settled at the table and I'll help Miss Elle put the sundaes together."

"Maybe we should wash hands first since she just came from school? Gigi, will you please help her with that?"

"I'm happy to do that," Gigi said. "In fact, Elle, why don't you go on and send that text you need to send and Miss Chloe can help me put our snack together. By the time you get back, those sundaes should be ready to eat."

Aidan had made it through surgery and was in the intensive care unit. He'd suffered a head injury as well as multiple broken bones, and the doctor had put him into a medically induced coma to bring down the brain swelling.

Now that he knew Aidan's condition, Daniel was torn. The bigger part of him, the part that wanted to do what was right, knew he should stay at the hospital in case his brother woke up, but hospitals freaked him out. He hated the smell. He hated the austere environment. He hated the dire reality of the place. Unless you worked there, you didn't go to the hospital unless something was gravely wrong. In his experience, when the people he loved entered the hospital, they didn't come out.

His parents. His grandmother. His wife.

He said a silent prayer that Aidan would recover and put an end to that grim streak.

The place made him anxious. And, yeah, as far as he was concerned, he couldn't get out of there fast enough. All selfishness aside, he needed to go get Chloe. He had imposed on Elle and her family enough. So, he left his contact information with the nurses and they had promised to call if Aidan woke up before Daniel could get back to the hospital tomorrow morning.

He exited the automatic double doors, at war with himself about leaving. There wasn't a damn thing he could do sitting around waiting for his brother to wake up. During visiting hours, he could sit with him, but the rest of the time, he'd be relegated to the waiting room or the hospital cafeteria.

Aidan would understand. In fact, he would probably kick his ass if he found out he'd been sitting there all day staring at the floor instead of taking care of Quindlin Brothers business. But even before he could do that, the first thing on his list was to take care of Chloe.

He had a full plate at work, and with Aidan in the hospital, he had no idea how he was going to get it all done and take care of a child. But Chloe was first priority. She had always been in school or day care since he and Aidan had become partners. But he didn't know which day care Aidan had put her in and he didn't know the first thing about selecting one—or finding a babysitter, for that matter. Really, he didn't want to leave her with a stranger. The hospital had released Aidan's belongings to him, so he had a key to his brother's house. The first thing he needed to do after he took an Uber to his truck, which was still parked near Rusty's, and picked up Chloe was go to his brother's house and put together a plan to make life as normal as possible for his niece.

Dread was a lead ball in his stomach. His gut reaction was that he didn't know how to take care of a five-year-old little girl. But he'd been around Aidan and Chloe enough to know he would manage. The one thing he wasn't sure about was how he would juggle the responsibility of full-time childcare with work and looking in on his brother.

As an architect, Aidan was in the office more than Daniel. If Chloe was home from school sick or on vacation, Aidan could work from home. The majority of Daniel's working hours were spent on jobsites. Jobsites were no place for a child.

Aidan was a good dad and made balancing work and fatherhood look effortless. Somehow, Daniel would make it work.

Chloe's mother had been out of the picture for years and Daniel didn't know where to begin looking to locate her or if it was what Aidan would want. It dawned on him that he wouldn't want to enlist the help of a woman who had walked away from her own child. She had left Aidan shortly after giving birth, leaving him with a newborn. She'd wanted no part of motherhood or marriage. Over the past five years, Aidan had perfected the art of being both mother and father to his daughter, putting her first and doing everything possible to give her a happy childhood.

Except for that damned motorcycle…

Daniel shook away the thought. The doctors said that his brother was young and healthy and they were hopeful that Aidan would recover…in time. But he wasn't out of the woods yet.

Now that Daniel was away from the hospital and could breathe in something other than that grim antiseptic smell, he could finally let down his wall and admit how damn scared he was at the thought of losing his brother.

Aidan wasn't out of the woods yet…

After the Uber driver dropped him off and he let himself into his truck, he took out some of his pent-up emotion on the steering wheel, hitting it with the side of his fist.

"Damn you, Aidan. How could you be so stupid? You had no business on a bike like that. Being a reckless idiot is my territory. Not yours, dumb-ass."

He punched at the steering wheel again, and for about the hundredth time, he wondered why it had to be Aidan lying in that bed and not him. Because he would gladly change places with him. Chloe needed her father. She depended on him.

Why did the drunk driver have to travel through

that intersection at the same time that Aidan had made the turn?

Would it have made a difference if he'd talked to his brother in the office a little bit longer? Kept him there... listened to what he was trying to tell him—something about Chloe and school and making cupcakes for her holiday party. Daniel had mocked him and called him Betty Crocker and then he'd cut him off and said he had to run. What if he'd tried to engage his brother in conversation for once instead of always having something more important to do? Would it have made any difference? Would he not be up there in the hospital in a medically induced coma fighting for his life?

When the moisture stung Daniel's eyes, he uttered a string of expletives and lowered his head onto the steering wheel, willing the weakness to pass. Before it did, his phone buzzed the arrival of a text and sent his heart into near cardiac arrest until he realized a split second later that if it was the hospital trying to get him, they would call, not text.

He turned over the screen and saw Elle's name.

Checking in to see if there was any news. We're fine here. So, no worries. Gigi and Chloe have become fast friends and are having a fun playdate.

Seeing her name was like a balm to Daniel's open wound. The thought of Chloe wrapped in the warm layers of Elle's family helped him regain his equilibrium. *Family*... He'd never dwelled on it, but now that one of his two living family members was in the hospital fighting for his life, that intangible seemed like the most rare and valuable thing in the world. Daniel had never been a praying man, but he closed his eyes and said a prayer for his brother to survive and recover and a prayer of thanks for the Boudreau-Clark family and their generous spirits. For the second time, they were there for him, extending selfless help.

Even though offering his remodeling skills at cost seemed inadequate, he would somehow find an adequate way to repay their kindness.

He picked up his phone and started typing.

Thanks for the update. I'm on my way to pick up Chloe. Tell Gigi I owe her. I owe you, too, Elle. Big time.

She texted right back. No one is keeping score.

He was tempted to text back and ask if that meant she'd stopped holding the Roger/wedding debacle against him. But that would be a cheap shot. She believed it was his fault that Roger had left her at the altar. All these years, he'd let her believe that. He wondered what would've happened if he hadn't gotten the call about Aidan. Would they have talked about what had happened before the wedding that made Daniel talk Roger into walking away? Would she have heard him out? Of course, learning the truth wouldn't have been any easier to swallow. Maybe it was just as well that she blamed him. If she could forgive him, maybe she didn't need to know the truth.

It was too bad that it took a tragedy to open lines of communication, but if any good came from Aidan's wreck, maybe this would be the catalyst that would help Elle and him put the past behind them once and for all.

Chapter Six

Daniel looked exhausted, Elle thought when she saw him standing in the lobby.

His handsome face looked drawn and pale, in sharp contrast with his dark hair and eyes. There were fine lines around his eyes that she hadn't noticed before. Of course, he'd faced the worst kind of stress today. If one of her sisters was in the intensive care unit, she probably wouldn't be able to function. Never mind how she would look. She'd be a mess. You wouldn't be able to pry her away from the hospital bedside, either. That wasn't a judgment. She knew the only reason Daniel was here right now was because of Chloe.

"Hi," she said. "How are you doing?"

He blinked. Obviously, he wasn't all there.

"Hey, umm, yeah…" He shrugged and shoved his

hands in his back pockets. "As good as can be expected? Where is Chloe?"

"She's out on the patio playing My Little Pony with Gigi."

The corners of his lips tugged upward.

"I'm impressed. Is Gigi sharing her own personal game?"

Elle laughed. At least he still had a sense of humor. Funny how people used to call him glib, when really humor was a life skill that carried people through hard times like he was facing now.

"You might say that. When Gigi learned it was Chloe's favorite game, they went to Target and bought it. They've been playing it all afternoon—dozens of times. I think it might be Gigi's new favorite hobby."

She motioned for him to follow her to one of the large picture windows where they had a good view of the game in progress on the back terrace.

"See what I mean? They're new BFFs."

Elle and Daniel stood next to each other, the quiet enveloping them. The only sound was the gentle tick-tock of the grandfather clock that was standing soldier straight on the adjacent wall. Elle stole a glance at him. The look in his eyes was heartbreaking. It took every ounce of restraint not to reach out and hug him. Because this big guy who was usually so cocky and sure of himself looked broken.

She crossed her arms to keep herself from doing something stupid, like invading his personal space. Something that could be misconstrued for something other than how she meant it.

"Chloe can stay here tonight if it would help you,"

she offered. "That way you can go back to the hospital tonight."

He did a double take. Squinted at her as if processing the offer and still coming up empty-handed on what to say.

"That's such a nice offer. Thank you. But I've already imposed on you enough. I'll take her home with me. First, we need to go by Aidan's house so I can pick up some things for her." He shrugged. "Maybe we'll stay there so she can go to sleep in her own bed. Do you think that would be better for her?"

"Maybe it would," Elle said. "Less change that way."

"I don't know what to tell her about her dad," he confessed. "What do I say? I mean, you're a teacher. I thought you might have some suggestions on what to say."

She nodded. "I do. But first, I need to let you know we already talked about it a little bit. I'm a stranger and when I showed up to pick her up rather than her dad, she wanted to know why. I told her that her father had to see the doctor. I didn't elaborate, but I answered her questions. She was mainly concerned about whether her dad would have to get a shot."

"Yeah?"

"That's a big deal to a five-year-old."

He nodded. "She's going to have more questions when Aidan doesn't come home tonight."

"She probably will," Elle said. "Answer her honestly and matter-of-factly, but don't get into complicated details."

When he didn't answer, she continued, "The most important thing is that she feels loved and safe. She needs to know that she will be taken care of while her father is away."

He nodded and raked a hand through his hair. "When I tell her about Aidan tonight, I'll make sure I lead with that. I want her to know everything will be okay.

"Aidan was planning on taking some time off while she was out of school on holiday break. I guess I will now. It will mean pushing out the inn's completion date. I hope your mom and Wiladean realize I have to do what's best for Chloe right now."

Daniel ran a hand over his eyes and back through his hair. It was clear that he was trying to figure it out as he went along. She could feel the angst rolling off him in palpable waves.

"Let me watch her, Daniel."

"Elle—"

"I know you need to take care of things tonight in your own way, but know that the offer stands. I teach kids not too much older than Chloe. If I look after her, it would free you up to go to the hospital. If you feel like working, you could bring her with you to the inn and work on the remodel. But only if you feel like it." Maybe she was imagining it, but it seemed like his mood shifted. He looked almost relieved.

"It's good of you to offer," he said. "But I can't work until I know that Aidan is out of danger."

Elle nodded. "The offer still stands for me to look after Chloe. Do you want me to come with you tonight to help you get Chloe settled? That way if she asks a question and you get stuck, you'll have me for moral support."

It was the least she could do. He was clearly suffering and doing the best that he could.

"You really are wonderful," he said.

He pulled her into a hug that felt familiar and somehow…right.

Maybe it was sheer exhaustion or maybe it was Elle's soothing presence, but Chloe was sound asleep within five minutes of them tucking her into bed. They'd ordered in a couple of pizzas for dinner—cheese for Chloe and pepperoni and mushroom for Elle and him. After dinner, Elle had helped Chloe with her bath and had gotten her ready for bed.

Just as Daniel had anticipated, at bedtime Chloe had asked about her dad and cried after they'd told her that he was hurt and had to sleep in the hospital until the doctor told him he could go home. She had asked if she could go see him and Daniel had told her he would ask the doctor. They would go as soon as the doctor said it was possible. He assured her that in the meantime, he was there to take care of her. They didn't let her cry herself to sleep alone. They both stayed in her bedroom with her, rubbing her back and answering all her questions and assuring her that they would be here for her.

It was a little awkward when she'd asked if Elle would be there in the morning when she woke up. Daniel had been grateful when Elle jumped in and took the lead. "No, sweetie, I have to go home tonight."

"Is that why you drove your own car?"

"It is. That way I can go home and your uncle Daniel can stay right here with you. He is going to bring you over to my house tomorrow morning. You and Gigi and

I can play all day long. You can teach me how to play My Little Pony. Doesn't that sound like fun?"

She'd nodded, momentarily placated. "Can I see my daddy tomorrow?"

Elle and Daniel locked gazes. "I'll ask the doctor tomorrow when I see him," he'd said, keeping his voice light and upbeat. It seemed to work because, with Princess Sweetie Pie tucked under her arm, Chloe's eyes had grown heavy, and she'd drifted off to sleep.

Silently, they left her bedroom. He didn't want Elle to leave, but he knew that if he didn't think fast, she would. She was already edging toward the door.

"It was a great idea to ask Chloe about her Christmas plans," he said, referring to their conversation during dinner. "Sometimes the obvious is right in front of you and you can't even see it. I'd totally forgotten that Aidan had signed her up for the holiday camp at the school the week before Christmas. I'll have to figure out the details. Like when it starts and the hours."

He liked this common ground they'd found tucking Chloe into bed together and making sure she felt safe and secure. Given everything, it was remarkable that Elle could put her animosity for him aside to help him help his niece. She was pretty remarkable. He'd always known it, but this was proof.

When there was so much on the line right now— Aidan's survival and prognosis, Chloe's comfort and well-being—it felt a little selfish to want to keep her here with him. But her calming presence was keeping him sane, too.

"You're really good with her, Daniel."

"I love her. I mean, she and Aidan are all I have."

"I'm so sorry this happened," she said.

He didn't know what to say and even if he did he doubted that he could push the words around the lump in his throat. She must've sensed his angst or maybe it was written all over his face, because she came to his rescue by offering her sweet smile.

"You've changed, haven't you?" she said.

His heart twisted in a way that had him inwardly vowing to prove her right. "I have changed," he said matter-of-factly. He didn't want to give her any reason to believe he was kidding. "The years have shown me what's important. That life is fragile. You don't always get a second chance."

"You have a point." She leaned her hip against the arm of the couch, settling into a half-standing, half-sitting position. She'd changed clothes since lunch. Now she was wearing jeans and a blue blouse that looked great with her eyes and worshipped her curves. He fisted his hands in his lap. She was so close the need to touch her was almost overwhelming. But he wouldn't give in to his primal urges. Not with Chloe in the next room.

Touching her because he could was something he would have done in his past life. That was when he was angry and resentful over losing his parents and having to move to Savannah, and he had taken out his anger by taking whatever he wanted, whenever he wanted it, without considering the consequences.

He stuffed his hands into his back pockets.

"What was the turning point for you?" she asked.

He shrugged.

"When did you decide that being the rebel wasn't the way to go?"

He studied her face for a moment, drinking in the contours and planes.

"There comes a time when you either choose to grow up or continue down that senseless, self-destructive path to nowhere. It also comes from finding something you're good at. Something you're passionate about."

As he stared at the Christmas tree in the corner of his brother's house, he thought about his late wife, Lana. She'd been good for him. In many ways she'd saved him. Most of all made him realize that the best way he could honor her after the aneurysm was to carry on with purpose, to not let his grief and anger make him self-destruct. That was part of the reason he'd come back to Savannah. To settle old scores, not through rage or even passive aggression, but through redemption. He learned fast that the best path to redemption was through self-worth.

"For me it was renovating old houses. I liked the irony of it. I used to break things, but now I fix them."

A look of dawning washed over her pretty face and he wanted to kiss her. The same way he had all those years ago.

"I never thought of it that way, but you're right."

She held his gaze and drew her bottom lip between her front teeth. He wondered if she was remembering that kiss and wanting to revisit it, as much as he did.

"Why did you feel the need to break up my wedding, Daniel?"

Well, there it was. The million-dollar question that he had both dreaded and wanted to plow into headfirst to clear the air. Because until they had talked about it and it was out of the way, there would be no moving forward in the direction he was certain they were destined to go.

"Are you sure you want to get into that now?" he asked.

Elle didn't want him to know she was ambivalent about knowing the truth. It had taken so long to get over the hurt and humiliation, bringing it up was like opening the wound all over again. But if she was truthful with herself, she knew the only way for the wound to truly heal was to bring everything out into the open.

"You're right. I'm sorry. Now probably isn't the time to talk about it," she said, suddenly second-guessing herself.

Why did she do that? She hated that about herself.

Make a decision and stick to it. Stop running away.

Daniel shrugged. "There's nothing for you to be sorry about. As far as I'm concerned, it's as good a time as any to talk about it. I'd really like to clear the air."

"It was insensitive of me to ask tonight, Daniel. You have more important things to worry about than dredging up the past. Especially when you need to find out about Chloe's Christmas camp."

He shook his head. "I'll find out if Chloe's friends are going to it and get in touch with their parents."

"That's a great idea," she said. "Since I'm a teacher, you'd think I would've thought of that."

"You helped a lot today," he said. "You really shouldn't be too hard on yourself."

She wondered if this was his way of subtly changing the subject to the camp so that they didn't have to talk about what happened at the wedding. She really shouldn't have brought it up.

She stood.

He was standing so close to her now. A frisson of awareness zinged through her and nearly took her breath away. She stepped back and butted up against the couch. He reached out and steadied her.

"You okay?" he asked.

"Yes. I'm fine."

I'm fine. You'll be fine. But why do I feel like you and I are anything but fine?

"If you can't find the friends' numbers, maybe her teacher could put you in touch with them," she said. "Even though the kids are on vacation, sometimes the teachers have workdays. Call tomorrow and check. Because you're right—kids usually go to camp together, don't they?"

She was rattling on. She sounded like an idiot.

"Let's see," he said. "The last time I sent my kids to camp— Oh, wait. I don't have kids."

He laughed. She did, too, but it sounded more like a nervous hiccup.

"Are you sure about that?" she asked.

"Yeah. I'm sure."

"Good to know."

She bit her bottom lip to keep herself from saying anything else stupid.

He reached out and lifted her chin so that she was looking him in the eyes.

The feel of his touch, the unwavering directness of his gaze heated her body.

"If you don't want to talk about the wedding, we

don't have to," he said, returning to the conversation they'd skirted with all the camp talk. "I won't lie to you, Elle. It's not pleasant. I mean, I wouldn't have intentionally messed with Roger's head if he'd been the fine, upstanding guy everyone thought he was. It didn't matter what *everyone* thought. You were the only one who mattered and I knew he didn't deserve you."

The way he was looking at her, with his eyes fiery and impassioned, in contrast with the gentle way he was touching her face—like he was holding something fragile—she thought he might lean in and kiss her. And the stupidest thing was that she would've let him.

She wanted him to.

But then he pulled away his hand and took a step back, putting some much needed space between them.

"The only thing I need for you to know is that I would never hurt you, Elle. Not on purpose. Not then. Not now. Not ever."

She blinked. Her lips parted slightly.

"Roger was cheating on me, wasn't he?"

Daniel didn't answer right away. He didn't have to. The look on his face said it all.

Until the wedding day, Daniel had been Roger's best friend. They'd kept in touch through Roger's college years at the University of Georgia. Even though Daniel didn't go to college, he'd spent more time in Athens, Georgia, than Elle had.

She hadn't been happy when Roger had asked Daniel to be his best man in their wedding. To her, Daniel had always been *that friend*, the one whose mission seemed intent on leading Roger astray. As if Roger, the man-child, was so naive and impressionable he could be led. For the first time it dawned on her that Roger was probably the one who had been doing the leading. He certainly had led her on a merry chase. For all these years it had been easier to blame Daniel than to accept the fact that Roger had been playing her for a fool long before the day he'd left her standing at the altar.

"I owe you an apology, Daniel."

"No, you don't."

"Yes, I do. You saved me from making the worst mistake of my life, but until now I blamed you for ruining everything. If it hadn't ended there, it would've ended eventually. It would've been messy, and even though Roger running out on me was pretty damn humiliating, it would've been more humiliating to be the wife who was the last to know about her husband's infidelities."

Pain knitted Daniel's brows. "I'm sorry it had to happen that way."

"Be honest with me. What happened the night before the wedding that made you so adamant about stopping the wedding? Did Roger cheat on me that night?"

"Elle." His voice was a warning.

"Daniel." Her voice was insistent.

"Did you not talk to Roger after he left?"

Elle shook her head. "I saw him once after the wedding. He apologized and said he realized too late that he didn't love me enough to spend the rest of his life with me." She shrugged. "But now I'm wondering if something else happened."

"After all this time do the details really matter?" he asked.

"Not the details. I need an answer to the burning question. For all these years, I wouldn't let myself go there. I wouldn't let myself see the truth, but now that I see it, I need to know for sure."

Daniel stood there looking at her with brown eyes that held so much emotion—not pity, but a kind of emotion that made her realize that he genuinely cared.

"Look, if it will make you feel better," she said, "telling me would justify what you did—nudging him at the altar. At least in my eyes—in my heart—it would justify it. Daniel, all these years you let people believe you were the bad guy. You've taken the fall for me getting left at the altar. I don't need details. I need a simple yes or no. Did Roger cheat on me the night before our wedding?"

Daniel took a deep breath and then nodded.

"Thank you for saving me from making the biggest mistake of my life." She felt herself moving toward him in slow motion, arms lifting, her hands touching his face, fingers threading through his curly brown hair. Her mouth covered his. He tasted achingly familiar and brand-new all at once. It was almost an out-of-body experience—as if she was watching the kiss unfold from above. When his arms closed around her and pulled her flush against his body, her world tipped on its axis and she fell tumbling into the promise conveyed in his kiss.

Chapter Seven

When Daniel awoke alone the next morning in a strange bed that wasn't his own, it took a minute for him to remember where he was—the guest room of his brother's house. The next thing he pondered was whether kissing Elle had been a dream. But he could still feel her mouth on his and still taste her on his lips. He knew without a doubt the kiss had happened. What he didn't know was how Elle would feel about it in the light of day.

She hadn't lingered afterward, which was probably a good thing because he wanted to keep kissing her. Hell, he hadn't wanted to stop there. But one kiss was not an all-access pass. Even if she'd wanted more, they both knew it shouldn't happen with Chloe in the next room.

It had been an awkward goodbye with them making

small talk about him bringing Chloe with him to the Forsyth Galloway Inn so he could go to the hospital and she, Zelda and Wiladean could watch Chloe.

But they hadn't talked any more about the wedding or what transpired before it. Obviously, she didn't want to hear the gory details of how Roger had awakened on his wedding day with a raging hangover and a stripper he'd met at the club where they'd celebrated his bachelor party.

Daniel had tried to stop him. When Roger started slurring his words and getting a little too cozy with his favorite—a redhead who had invited him on stage to play the submissive in her tribute to *Fifty Shades of Grey*—Daniel had intervened and told the woman Roger was getting married. He'd gone as far as shepherding Roger to the car and driving home and dumping his drunk ass into his hotel bed. But obviously somewhere during the night, the pair had exchanged contact information. They'd ended up exchanging more than that. When Roger didn't answer his phone the next morning, Daniel had gone to his hotel, prepared to pour a gallon of coffee down his sorry throat and stuff him under a cold shower and into his wedding tux. That was when he'd found him passed out with the woman in his bed. He was supposed to be getting married in two hours.

Daniel had tried to talk him out of going through with it. He'd tried to persuade him to call Elle and do the right thing by canceling or at least postponing until Roger could work through whatever it was that was compelling him to act this way. Daniel's argument was that if he wasn't ready to get married, he shouldn't get married.

No judgment. Just facts. If he still had a penchant for strippers—a penchant that went beyond casually watching them—then maybe he needed to rethink taking a vow where he'd pledge to forsake all others except for Elle until death did them part.

After the redhead left and Roger showered, he'd dressed in his tux and had insisted on going through with the wedding. Until it came down to the moment when he had to look Elle in the eyes and take his vows.

Thank God for that moment of clarity. Because until Roger bolted, Daniel had thought he was going to go through with it.

Elle didn't need to know that. He would've spared her the hurt even if she'd insisted on hearing the details. And she could be pretty damn persuasive. But she seemed satisfied with the abridged version of the story. Maybe it was wishful thinking because Daniel had been in love with her since the first moment he'd seen her at Savannah Country Day, but it finally felt like the path to each other—that had always been blocked—was finally clear.

He wasn't going to kid himself. With all that was happening with Aidan, if this was going to work out, it might take a while longer. But he'd waited this long. He was willing for them to take their time so they could finally get it right. And they still had hurdles to clear.

He hoped Elle wasn't having regrets about the revelation and the kiss.

The kiss had come on the tail of such an emotional revelation that he needed to not get carried away or read anything more into it. It might have been nothing more than her way of coming to terms with the confirmation that her ex-fiancé had cheated the night before their wedding. It might even have been a reflexive payback. Which could've been a thank-you to him or a private *So there, I'll kiss your best friend* directed at Roger, who would never know it happened. Daniel had spoken to Roger exactly once after he'd left Elle standing at the altar and Daniel holding the scapegoat bag. Then the weasel had disappeared into his new life.

Right now, Daniel needed to focus on the day ahead. He needed to go by the hospital to check on Aidan. An uneasy feeling nagged in his gut. No one had called, but rather than assume no news was good news—or at least it wasn't bad news—he called the hospital.

Aidan was stable. That was great news.

For a moment, he considered not going to the hospital. He loved his brother but holding vigil at his bedside wouldn't do anyone any good. But he knew he should go. That was what good people did. They went to the hospital. But it was so damn hard.

Chloe was still sleeping when he got up. He quickly showered and surveyed the food situation in his brother's kitchen to see what kind of breakfast he could scrounge up.

As he started to open the refrigerator, a piece of paper tacked to the door with a couple of kids' alphabet magnets caught his eye.

Daniel took the paper off the refrigerator and studied it. It was a flyer for a weeklong holiday camp at Savannah Country Day. *Well, hell.* It had been right there all the time. He hadn't noticed it because they had ordered in pizza and he hadn't paid attention to the collage of papers on his brother's fridge last night when he'd gotten Chloe some juice to have with dinner.

It was for one week, but it didn't start until the week before Christmas. If he could rely on Elle until camp started, it would buy him some time until Chloe started back at school after the new year. Maybe by that time, Aidan would be out of the hospital.

Within the hour, he had loaded Chloe into his truck, buckled her into the booster seat that Elle had taken out of her car and headed to the Forsyth Galloway Inn.

"Look what I found," Daniel said as he walked into the Forsyth's kitchen, clutching Chloe's hand and holding up a piece of paper with his free hand.

He looked so darned hot, Elle thought. What was it about a big strong man holding a child's hand that made her insides turn to mush? She'd seen plenty of fathers holding their children's hands and none had awakened her lady parts like this.

It was Daniel. That kiss last night after the confession that she'd pried out of him had set her free.

And she'd been nervous about how he would act this morning. She worried that when she was admitting to herself that yes, she had a thing for her former nemesis, Daniel Quindlin, who hadn't ruined her life but in his own stoic way had saved her from making the worst mistake, maybe he wouldn't see her in quite the same way that she saw him.

Yet, here he was, smiling and thrusting a piece of paper at her, acting as if he couldn't be happier to see her.

"What is that?" she asked.

"Chloe's camp."

"Seriously? You found it?"

He nodded. "It was hanging right there on the refrigerator in plain sight. It was sort of collaged in among the other stuff Aidan had up there, but it jumped out at me this morning."

She took the paper from him and read it. "Oh, it's an art camp. Chloe, do you like art?"

The little girl nodded. "Princess Sweetie Pie and I like to draw and paint."

Elle returned the paper to Daniel. "I do, too. I have a feeling that you and I are going to have a lot of fun while your uncle Daniel works around here today."

"Uncle Daniel, are you staying here all day?" Chloe asked.

"I sure am. I will be right here if you need me."

Chloe frowned and hugged her white cat.

"I thought you were going to visit my daddy and ask the doctor when I can go see him."

Daniel's gaze snared Elle's for a moment and she gave a quick nod, trying to telegraph that it was fine for him to go and check on his brother and that she was happy to look after Chloe.

"It's probably a good idea for you to go touch base with the doctor and get an update on Aidan."

"I called this morning. They said he'd stabilized."

She sensed a shift in his mood, a hesitancy. She couldn't quite put her finger on what was wrong, but something was.

"Chloe and I have a lot planned," she said to lighten the mood. "So, go ahead. We probably won't even miss you."

Again, Daniel snared Elle's gaze. "I hope *you'll* miss me."

And bam, there it was again, that feeling that had her heart twisting and her lady parts singing. She needed to be careful because she wasn't sure what those rogue feelings were about and she would wager that he wasn't completely clear, either.

"I will miss you, Uncle Daniel. You will come back as soon as you see Daddy, right?"

There was something uneasy in his smile. In fact, it seemed as if he was only making the effort to smile for Chloe's sake. If not for his upbeat entrance this morning and the bit about hoping she would miss him, Elle might have worried that his mood was personal. But here she was overthinking it again.

"Actually, I'm not sure if I'll get to go today," he said. "But I'll ask the doctor when I talk to him."

"You're not going to the hospital?" Elle asked.

"We'll see. When I spoke to the nurse, she said they'll call me if there's a change—"

"Good morning," Gigi called as she pushed through the kitchen doors.

"Good morning." Elle looked at her watch, glad for the diversion. "You're up early this morning. It's only 7:30."

"I have a very good reason to be up all bright-eyed and bushy-tailed." She looked at Chloe and the little girl broke into a fit of giggles.

"Princess Sweetie Pie has bright eyes and a bushy tail, Gigi. See?"

She held up the cat for Gigi to inspect. "My goodness, look at that. She sure does."

Gigi bent down so that her ear was at the level of the cat's mouth. "What's that, Princess Sweetie Pie? You want to play the My Little Pony game?" Chloe's eyes got big and she moved the cat so its head bobbed up and down.

"Of course, I'd love to play, Princess Sweetie Pie," Gigi said. "I'll see if Chloe wants to play, too."

The child bounced up and down with excitement. "Yes! Yes! I want to play."

Gigi took the little girl's hand and shot a knowing smile first to Elle and then to Daniel and back to Elle.

Could she be more obvious?

"Sorry to leave you two alone, but Chloe, Princess Sweetie Pie and I have big plans. You two entertain each other."

She winked and then followed Chloe, who was already halfway out the kitchen door.

Elle heard Gigi greet some guests who were staying at the inn, but she couldn't hear the conversation through the swinging door. For a moment, she considered going out to see if she could help. But it was her mother's day to set out breakfast and tend to the guests. She knew the real reason she was tempted to go out there was that she was standing here with Daniel, with the feel of last night's kiss still fresh on her lips, and she had that same uneasy feeling in her stomach she'd had yesterday, when Gigi had skipped out on their lunch plans and left her alone with Daniel. Once again, it was obvious that her grandmother was doing her best to push them together. Not to mention, all of Daniel's walls seemed to go up whenever they talked about him going to the hospital. She had no idea what that was about. All she knew was things felt a little awkward.

"What time is the crew arriving?" she asked.

Daniel glanced at the clock on his phone. "In about an hour and a half. I told them to get here around nine o'clock. Why?"

"Are you going to the hospital before they arrive?"

"Since Aidan is stable, I thought I'd wait and go at noon."

There it was again. She sensed him tense up ever so slightly. "Then that leaves plenty of time for a quick walk. I love Forsyth Park in the morning. Will you walk with me? It would do us both some good to get some fresh air. I can fill up a couple of to-go cups to take with us."

She took down two travel mugs from the cupboard. He liked his coffee black. She remembered that from the hospital yesterday. So much had changed since yesterday. It felt like months. She knew his kiss, the feel of his lips on hers and his hands on her body, but there was so much more she didn't know about this man.

Pouring a cup of coffee for a man in the morning suddenly seemed very intimate. For a moment the image of Daniel lying next to her in bed, naked and sleep-warmed as morning light streamed in through the window played out like a movie in her mind. Even though her better judgment screamed foul, she could not unsee—unfeel—this vision. Even though she knew it was futile because her time in Savannah was temporary. She was going back to Atlanta…eventually.

She tried to ignore the voice that said, *Since you're*

leaving...what could a fling hurt? Get him out of your system.

She blinked away the thought.

"I could definitely use a cup right now," he said.

She poured the steaming liquid into two cups... *naked in bed drinking coffee the morning after a night of good sex.*

What would it be like to be with Daniel?

Stop.

Not going to happen.

Until it does.

They headed out the kitchen door and walked up Hall Street toward Forsyth Park. The light was that soft-filtered silver and liquid gold that streamed through the Spanish moss and dripped through the live oak branches making the park with its Christmas decorations look ethereal. It was pleasantly warm so they didn't need jackets and just humid enough to make the breeze feel like a caress.

"This is my favorite time of day," she said, breaking the silence when they reached Whitaker Street and paused for the burst of traffic to pass on the one-way street.

"It's nice," he said. "My office is in an old Victorian on the other side of the park. I like to run in the park before work. There's a full bath so I can shower and get ready for the day. So, you're an early morning person, too?"

"As a teacher, I don't really have a choice."

"Do you like teaching art?" Her gut tightened at the reminder that she no longer had a job teaching art. She steered him toward the Forsyth Park Garden of Fragrance, which was one of her favorite spots. Located on the west side of the park, a few yards away from the fountain, the fragrant garden was surrounded by walls on three sides with an ornate iron gate along the front.

"It's…fun," she said as she pushed open the iron gates and stepped inside.

"But?"

"But what?" She settled on the stone bench. Daniel sat beside her. His thigh touching hers.

"Your answer had a *but* on the end. *It's fun…but,*" he said.

"I didn't say that."

"You didn't have to. It was implied by your voice."

"You're perceptive. But the situation is a little complicated."

"So, tell me about it," he said. "I can handle complicated."

She bit her bottom lip. "I'm sure you can, but that's not why I asked you to walk with me."

"Uh-oh. That sounds ominous."

She smiled. "I'll make a deal with you. If you'll tell me why you don't want to go to the hospital, I'll tell you why my situation is complicated."

He tensed again. His leg pulled away from hers as he focused on the rim of his cup. "What makes you think I don't want to go to the hospital?"

"First of all, because you won't look at me when we talk about Aidan and the hospital."

He locked gazes with her. "I'm looking at you."

He was afraid. She could see it in his eyes. She shifted so that she was turned toward him and her knee was touching his. "Mostly, because every time

I've mentioned the hospital you look terrified, like you want to bolt."

"Running isn't how I handle things," he said.

She wanted to challenge him and point out that his deciding to work this morning rather than being there with his brother had sure seemed like running. Or at the very least, avoidance. But she didn't say it.

"Okay, maybe I'm reading you wrong," she said, "but it seems to me that every time someone mentions the hospital, you look a little freaked out. It seems like you and your brother have a pretty good relationship. I'm trying to figure out why you don't…"

Her words trailed off as his eyes searched her face. He looked a little panicked. She decided maybe she shouldn't push it. Instead, she let the silence stretch between them for a moment.

"Just because I don't spend every waking hour at his bedside doesn't mean I don't care."

He sounded defensive. She really hadn't meant to upset him.

"I'm not judging, Daniel. So, please don't be angry."

"I'm not angry."

"If you're not then will you hear me out?"

He nodded.

"Even though he's in a coma, he might be able to hear your voice, or sense your presence. Knowing you're there might make him stronger."

He bent forward, placing his elbows on his knees, looking down, very much the same way he'd sat at the hospital. She prepared herself for him to get up and leave. So, she stayed as quiet and still as she could while he sat next to her.

"I don't mean to not do right by Aidan," he finally said. "It's because hospitals aren't my favorite place. Every time there's been an emergency that involved a hospital, the odds have never turned out in my favor. The person I love has never come out alive. My folks were in a car wreck when I was going into my senior year of high school. They never made it out alive. My grandmother had a stroke and they couldn't fix her. My wife had an aneurysm, but they couldn't save her. Now Aidan is in there fighting for his life. He and Chloe are all the family I have left."

He shrugged.

Wife? Daniel had been married? It was the first she'd heard of it, but it didn't feel like the right time to ask him about it.

"I'm sorry." She thought about reaching out and taking his hand. "I didn't know that's what it was about."

"Did you think I didn't feel like going?"

"No, Daniel. There was no judgment. I really didn't know what it was about, but I could sense something." She held up her hands. "No judgment, I promise. However, think about this. You not going to the hospital doesn't change the fact that Aidan's there. It's such good news that he's stabilizing, but you still need to talk to him. You need to go see him. If not for yourself, for Chloe. And, of course, if you need help with Chloe or someone to go with you to the hospital to help you through it—my family and I are here for you. I'm here for you."

"Thanks, Elle. You're lucky to have them—your family." He curved his lips into a smile, but the sentiment didn't reach his eyes.

She nodded.

"Your grandmother has always been good to me. She took in my family after the fire and now she's making Chloe feel so safe and happy. All the years in between, she's been decent and kind to me. She could see beyond the hooligan I might have been when I was a teenager to the person I've become. And it was because of her kindness that people in this community stopped trying to shut me out."

"Gigi has always been a kind person," Elle said, but it felt so inadequate.

And Daniel had been married.

"You're a kind person, too, Elle." he said. "I haven't abandoned my brother. But the truth is, going in and holding constant vigil at his bedside while he's hooked up to tubes and machines is hard."

"I'll go with you."

He nodded. "That might help. How about today when I take a lunch break?"

"You've got it."

"Now you need to tell me about the complication that's keeping you from loving your job."

"I did make that deal, didn't I?"

"You did."

She sipped her coffee. It burned her lips because it was still a little too warm in the insulated mug.

"I didn't know you'd been married." The words fell out before she could stop them. She couldn't make herself apologize for prying or say he didn't have to talk about it. Even though she wanted to fill the silence that was hanging between them, she couldn't say anything.

Finally, Daniel spoke. "I was married for seven

months. Her name was Lana. She was..." He smiled a sad smile and shook his head. "She was electricity and sunshine and everything that was good. She kind of reminded me of you in a way."

His admission took away Elle's breath.

"You said it was an aneurysm?"

Daniel nodded. "Yep."

"How long has it been?"

"Five years."

"Daniel, I'm so sorry."

"Don't be. It won't bring her back. I mean, it sucks. All the way around. You love someone and in the blink of an eye they're gone."

His eyes glistened with unshed tears, but he didn't look away from her.

Never had a man been so open and vulnerable with her.

She didn't know what to say. She didn't feel like she had the right. She'd never lost anyone she loved— not to death. The thought sent a cold shiver coursing through her.

Then Daniel did the most unexpected thing. He put his arm around her and held her close. It was almost as if he was comforting her, when it should've been the other way around.

"So, there you go. Lana's one of the reasons I've changed. I've learned that life doesn't give you many second chances. When it does, you better take it."

He bent down and brushed her lips with a feather-light kiss. Then he said, "Now, it's your turn. Tell me about your job. Why is it not fun anymore?"

"Oh. It seems so trivial after what you told me. So, no. Never mind."

"A deal is a deal. In fact, I told you two things I don't like to talk about. Your turn."

"Okay." She shrugged. His arm was still around her and she realized there was nowhere on earth she'd rather be. "The reason it's not fun is I don't have a job teaching art anymore. Thanks to lack of funding, they had to eliminate my position. The powers that be place art low on the priority list. So, there you go. Not fun."

"Does that mean you're staying in Savannah?"

"I don't know. Uh, probably not. I mean, my life is in Atlanta. But I may have to go wherever I can find a job."

"If it makes a difference," he said, leaning closer and toying with a strand of her hair, "I'd love for you to stay. Will you give me a chance to try and talk you into moving back?"

His breath was hot on her temple. And her breath hitched as she sighed at the closeness.

Oh, how she wanted him in her personal space.

Then his lips skimmed her cheek, and Elle tilted back her head, looking up at him. His eyes were hungry and hooded, and the next thing she knew, his lips were brushing hers again.

This time, the kiss started slow and soft, then ignited into greedy hunger that made her part her lips and lean in to deepen it. Her stomach swooped and she fisted her hands into the back of his shirt, clinging to him as if her next breath depended on him.

They'd come so far—stolen kisses. Unfaithful grooms. Ruined weddings. Injured brothers. The only thing that mattered now was how well their bodies fitted together

He used his key fob to open the passenger-side door. Before he opened it for her, he said, "No, I haven't. We need to fix that."

"I'll bet Gigi would watch Chloe for us."

"And what are you going to tell her? About us, I mean?"

As she looked up into his eyes, the setting sun reflected the various shades of blue, green and silver in her irises. He thought if he could freeze this moment in time he would be happy and fulfilled—or so his heart said. His body begged to differ. His body wanted to claim her for its own. To unwrap her like she was the Christmas present he'd been waiting for all his life and hold her so that their naked bodies were so close it was hard to tell where he ended and she began…and then he would bury himself inside her—

"Tomorrow night, my sister Kate and I are having dinner with our mom and Gigi. I guess that would be a good time to let my family know that some things have changed between us."

Chapter Eight

"Do pirates really live here, Uncle Daniel?" Chloe's eyes were huge as she looked around the busy restaurant after the hostess seated her, Elle and him at their table at the famous Pirates' House restaurant.

The guy dressed like a pirate trolling guests out in front of the place had done a good job setting the tone for this world-famous destination. He'd certainly grabbed Chloe's attention.

"Sure, they do," Daniel said. "The pirate who was talking to you outside lives here. It's his house."

The place was touristy and he normally didn't go for something like this, but it seemed like a fun, family-friendly place that he and Elle could take Chloe before their trip to the art supply store to get her easel.

"Why does he let all these people inside his house?" Chloe asked. "They will eat all his food."

Elle and Daniel laughed. "He has lots of food and he likes to share." Elle pointed to the menu. "See all the different choices. What would you like to eat?"

"I'll bet I can guess what you want to eat, matey," Daniel said in his best pirate's accent.

Chloe nodded and giggled as she hugged her stuffed white cat.

"I'll bet you want a heaping kettle of catfish. Am I right?"

"Nooo!" Chloe said. "Guess again."

"Shiver me timbers, then it has to be the jambalaya. Yeah, that's what the little missy will be wanting. Bring her a big pot of jambalaya."

"Nooo!" she laughed. "I don't know what that is, silly."

"The name is Black Beard to you, silly missy. Black Beard the pirate."

"Your name isn't Black Beard, it's Uncle Daniel, and Princess Sweetie Pie wants chicken fingers. And French fries."

"Ahhh, I don't know, that be the dish that's reserved only for the most special pirate princesses. Are ye a special pirate princess?"

"Yes, I am, and so is Princess Sweetie Pie."

"Well, then, chicken fingers ye both shall have, but only if ye draw me a pretty picture."

"I will!" Chloe plucked a purple crayon out of the small basket that the hostess had left on the table and started coloring the picture on the place mat.

That was when Daniel noticed an older woman at the table next to them beaming at them.

"She's adorable. How old is she?"

"I'm five." Chloe fanned out the five fingers on the hand that wasn't holding the crayon. She checked her hand as if she was making sure she had the right number.

"You seem like a very smart and well-behaved young lady," the woman said as she and her party scooted their chairs back and prepared to leave. "It warms the heart to see parents so engaged in their child. You are the most beautiful little family."

"Thank you," Daniel said.

He flashed a knowing smile at Elle, to see how she would react.

When she smiled and thanked the woman, too, for that moment in time, looking at her sitting across the table from him, next to Chloe, he felt like they were a family. Daniel soaked up what it would be like to be married to Elle and out to dinner with their child.

It felt *right*.

"What?" Elle said, smiling at him.

He shook his head, grinning back at her.

"This place makes me think of the architecture tours you were talking about offering your guests," he said, needing to ground himself in more substantial thoughts than pretending to be married to her.

"How so?" she asked.

"It's not only the oldest building in Savannah, but it's considered the oldest house in all of Georgia."

"I've heard that, but—okay, I'll confess. Can you believe that even though I was born and raised here, this is the first time I've ever been to the Pirates' House?"

"Get out," he said, leaning in. "I thought this place was mandatory for all natives."

"No, it's mandatory for all tourists," she said.

"Which makes it a must-see for your architecture tour. The historic restaurant and tavern area of the place were built in the 1750s, but that small building that we passed on the way in, the Herb House, was built in the 1730s. That's some pretty significant architectural history."

"It sure is," she said. "It's pretty impressive that you know so much about it. Were you always interested in architecture?"

He shook his head. "I don't know. Maybe I was, but I didn't realize it. If I'd always been interested in it, I probably would've gone to college and studied architecture. Like Aidan."

"It's never too late."

He leaned back so that his back was flush against the chair. "I have too much on my plate already with my business. There's not a lot of extra time, which is a good problem to have. Plus, I think I'd probably prefer building over designing, but I think it's knowing the design end—or at least the features that are specific to the original houses of Savannah—that sets me apart from the competition."

Elle held up her hands. "You've convinced me. I think it's cool that you're into the history because it interests you."

It was crazy, but the way she tilted her head made him think about their history—about the first time he saw her, about that time when she was trying to teach him grammar and he leaned in and kissed her. He wanted to do it again and would have, right there in the middle of the Pirates' House, if Chloe hadn't been sitting there.

"Will you give me your architectural tour of Savannah?"

He blinked. Her request caught him off guard.

"Um… I don't really have a tour, per se."

"Maybe one evening we can walk around and you can point out some of your favorites."

Normally, he would've made a joke about finder's fees or something equally lame, but he didn't want to spoil the moment.

"That sounds like a date."

"It's about time you made some time to see me." Elle hugged her sister Kathryn and laughed to soften the reprimand so that Kate knew she was kidding—sort of.

"I got back into town last night," Kate said, hitching her shoulder bag back into place. "I was on a weeklong cruise to the Bahamas. I got in late last night."

"Well, that explains why you're so tanned and why you haven't been returning my calls," Elle said as they walked through the lobby on their way to the kitchen. She waved at a couple who was spending their honeymoon at the Forsyth. They were dressed up and looked like they were heading out for a night out on the town.

"Right, I didn't have cell service on the ship and I didn't think you'd want me to call you at two o'clock this morning when I got home. You'll have to catch me up on everything I missed while I was gone."

"Oh my gosh. Where do I start?" Elle said as she made a mental list of everything—coming home because she lost her job. Daniel. Aidan's accident. *Dan-*

iel. Keeping Chloe. *Daniel*. Their mom and Gigi being at odds over the renovation and the new direction that Zelda wanted to take with the inn... *Daniel*.

From her shoulder bag, Kate pulled a bottle of red wine, a small bottle of rum, which she told Elle she'd brought back from the islands, some brandy, a carton of orange juice and several pieces of fruit. She lined them up on the table. "I thought I'd make some sangria for us to drink during this family meeting Mom and Gigi have called. Do you know where Gigi keeps the pitchers?"

"I'll look for one," Elle offered.

"Thanks, and if you'll hand me that cutting board, I'll get started cutting up the fruit so it can marinate in the brandy."

As Elle pulled open the cupboard doors, she said, "Didn't you use to date Aidan Quindlin?"

Kate snorted. "I don't know if you'd call it dating." She grimaced. "He had a crush on me in high school and asked me to the prom. It sort of ended badly and it was my fault. I'll own that much. I should've never agreed to go to the dance with him. Why?"

"He had a bad motorcycle accident last week."

"Oh, no. That's terrible. But Aidan Quindlin rides a bike? He was always such a nerd."

"Kate!" Elle said as she set a glass pitcher on the table. "That's so mean. He got hurt pretty badly."

Kate covered her mouth with her hand and looked truly contrite. "Oh, wow, I'm so sorry to hear that. Is he going to be okay?"

"He's in a coma at Memorial University Hospital, but as of yesterday, his prognosis took a turn for the better. They think he's going to be okay, eventually."

"A coma?" Kate looked taken aback. "I'm glad he's going to be okay. I think I'll go see him tomorrow. When are visiting hours?"

Elle told her. Kate pursed her lips and squinted at her sister, knife poised midair. "How is it that you know so much about Aidan's condition and visiting hours?"

Elle braced herself. "I was with his brother, Daniel, when he got the call about the accident."

Kate set down the knife and held up both palms like a traffic cop commanding an intersection. "Whoa! Hold up there. Back up. What the hell were you doing with Daniel Quindlin?"

Elle's stomach tightened, then flipped.

Here we go.

"Having lunch." She said it as if she was discussing one of her high school girlfriends, not the guy whom both of her sisters hated on her behalf. Even though she was nervous to tell Kate about the unexpected turn of events, she was eager to talk about them and their new…friendship? She hesitated to call it a relationship because everything was so new, and had been driven by such volatile emotions, but it was definitely more than friendship. Friends did not kiss like that or have daydreams about doing so much more. She didn't really know what to call it, what to call them. She wished she didn't have to slap a label on them at this point. Because that was the fastest way to kill the passion.

"Um…lunch?" Kate blew out a breath that made her lips buzz for a second. "I'm confused. I think you need to start from the beginning."

And so Elle did. She told her sister how she'd lost her job and come home. She told her about seeing Daniel jogging in the park and how he'd appeared in the Forsyth lobby a little while later.

"Did you know Mom and Gigi are renovating the inn?" Elle asked.

"Mom and Gigi are renovating the inn? What? I go away for a week and everything turns upside down."

"Apparently the reno plans have been perking longer than a week. By the time I found out, Daniel was already on board as the general contractor."

Kate did a double take. "Are you kidding me? I see them at least two or three, sometimes four times a week—depending on who needs her hair done—and they failed to mention any of this to me? Nice."

"So, it's not just me," Elle said. "It feels like they've been a little sneaky about the way they've handled this?"

"Who's being sneaky about what?" Zelda breezed into the kitchen carrying a manila file folder.

The sisters looked at each other. Then Elle looked away. She wished she'd had enough time to tell Kate the rest of the story about Daniel. Now she wasn't sure if she wanted to open the can of worms in front of everyone.

She hated herself for thinking of them as a *can of worms*. Maybe it proved that she needed more time to process everything.

Kate put her hands on her hips. "To start with, you and Gigi. What's this about you hiring Daniel Quindlin to remodel the inn?"

Kate spat out his name as if it might leave a bad taste in her mouth. Regret tugged at Elle's heart. She should have told her sister.

Zelda set her folder on the table and then checked her posture. "And why is that a problem?"

Kate glared at their mother. "Are you kidding?" She turned to Elle. "She's kidding, right? Because any mother who would hire the guy who wrecked her own daughter's wedding would be—"

"Elle knows that we hired Daniel. In fact, Elle seems to not only be fine with it, but she seems to have made her peace with Daniel. Kate, you can't live in the past. If you do, you'll end up being old and bitter."

"Who's old and bitter?" Gigi entered the kitchen holding several brown paper bags, which she set on the table. "I hope you're not talking about me."

"No, we're talking about Kate," Zelda said.

Gigi fisted her hands on her hips. "Why do you think Kate is old and bitter? She's young and fabulous."

"Because she's still holding a grudge against Daniel Quindlin." Zelda said.

"Kate, honey, why are you bitter about Daniel Quindlin? I thought you dated his brother. Oh, and say, did you hear that Aidan's in the hospital? He was in quite a nasty crash. You should go see him."

"Yes, Gigi, I heard about Aidan. I'm very sorry that happened. But that aside, how could you do this to Elle? Hiring Daniel Quindlin, of all people. Elle is broken-hearted over this."

Enough was enough.

"I'm not brokenhearted. I think I'm falling in love with Daniel Quindlin," Elle announced, surprising herself for flying right past friendship and dating and landing on the L-word.

Three pairs of eyes gaped at her and three mouths fell wide open.

"What the hell?" Kate was the first to respond. She looked seriously affronted.

"Oh, my." Zelda drawled, confusion clouding her pretty green eyes.

"I knew it," Gigi celebrated, clapping her hands as if her team had won the World Series.

But Daniel didn't know it, and neither had Elle, until she'd blurted it like the words had been caged inside her and had clawed their way out.

"Well, I mean we're seeing each other," Elle amended.

"Since when?" Kate demanded.

"Since last week."

One week. Elle realized how ridiculous it must seem. She'd spent years detesting this man and after spending a week with him, she thought she was falling in love?

"I don't understand," Kate said and busied herself putting together the sangria.

"I don't understand it, either," Elle said. "But it's happening. Daniel and I had a chance to talk about things and it helped me realize that he's not a bad guy."

Kate made a sound that was somewhere between a tsk and a snort.

"He was a pretty rough dude in school, Elle."

"Says the girl who used to like to dress up like Columbia in Rocky Horror Picture Show and act out the part at the midnight movies on Saturday nights when you were in high school, but that isn't who you are now."

"Thank God," Zelda murmured.

"Mom," Elle and Kate said in unison.

"We don't hold it against her," Elle said, making the point to her mom and grandmother. "Do we?"

"I make it a personal rule not to hold any kind of grudge," Gigi said. "I try to talk to people if we have a problem."

"You talked to Daniel?" Elle asked.

"Of course I did," Gigi said. "I didn't dig into the past, but I didn't have to. I figured that if you and Roger were meant to be, nothing could keep you apart."

Gigi's shrug filled in the missing words, *And we all know how that turned out.*

"I consider myself a pretty good judge of character," Gigi said. "When I started shopping around for a general contractor, I learned that Daniel Quindlin was the best. I figured, why should I settle for someone second-rate when I could have Quindlin Brothers, the very best, refurbish our family home? Besides, I sense that Daniel has always had a thing for you, Elle. It took guts to stand up there at your wedding and do what he did in front of all those people. When Roger ran, I knew he didn't deserve you. I always thought he was a little too sneaky and slick for his own good. And yours, too."

"I guess that's one way to look at it," Kate said. "Is that how you feel, Elle?"

"Amazingly so," Elle said. Admitting it made her stomach hurt a little. But she still wanted to walk back her confession of falling in love. And, okay, if she thought about it too hard, in real-world terms, she had the urge to run away and go back to her safe, if not somewhat boring, life in Atlanta. But at the same time, she was aware that the urge to run was a symptom of the post-traumatic stress she'd suffered after Roger.

And how was that working out for her? She'd let herself edge toward a new relationship exactly once since Roger. She'd been the one to end things because there was no chemistry—to preempt things—before she'd even given Heath a chance.

She and Daniel had mad chemistry and after announcing it to her family she was getting cold feet.

Was that what she wanted? To be alone? Was that how she wanted to live?

"In the spirit of full disclosure," Elle said, "this is new. Obviously. Daniel and I are still trying to figure things out. I didn't mean to throw around the 'love' word wantonly, so maybe you could keep that part to yourself. It's premature."

"Oh, brother." Kate rolled her eyes. "Do you love him or not? I need to know whose side I'm on."

"Thank you for being on my side, Kate," Elle said.

"We're all on your side," Gigi said.

"I need a drink," Zelda said, eyeing the pitcher of sangria in which Kate was muddling the fruit. Zelda hopped up and got four wine glasses from one of the cupboards. "Take your time and don't let anyone rush you into anything. Being alone isn't necessarily a bad thing."

Elle knew her mother was thinking of her divorce. She didn't talk about it very often.

Fred Clark had left Zelda when the girls were in elementary school. An alcoholic, her father had been unemployed more often than he'd held a job. Zelda finally gave up trying to collect child support. She'd decided making a clean break was better for her daughters than the occasional check from Fred. Everything was fine for a couple of years until Fred sued for half interest in the Forsyth Galloway Inn.

He'd lost, but his stunt had inspired Gigi to have a lawyer strengthen the terms of the trust protecting the inn from husbands of future generations succeeding in pulling a similar stunt.

Ever the optimist, Gigi had said being able to add extra protections to the ownership of their beloved inn had been the silver lining in an otherwise heartbreaking relationship. Zelda saw it as a heartbreaking ending. She hadn't been the same since the divorce. Even though Fred had lost his pursuit for half the value of the inn, it was as if he had stolen Zelda's spirit.

"I'm glad I brought the sangria," Kate said. "I think we all need it."

"Listen to me, everyone," Elle said in her teacher's voice. "I may have gotten a little caught up in the moment when I said I was falling in love with Daniel. Seeing him in this new light has been…nice. Freeing. But when I step back, I have to factor in that this is an emotional time for him with Aidan in the hospital. And I hadn't planned on staying when I came home. I haven't heard back from the county about whether or not they have a place for me. If they do, I'll go back to Atlanta.

"Daniel's business is here. My life is there. That's all we need to say about it for now. Gigi and Mom, you two are the reason we're all together tonight. You called the meeting. The floor is yours."

Zelda and Gigi, who had been setting out an array of appetizers that she had picked up from Hitch restaurant on Drayton Street, exchanged what Elle might have considered wary glances, but she was trying not to jump to conclusions anymore. Forming her own opinion before hearing the facts had been holding her hostage for years.

"I wish Jane could be here with us tonight," Gigi said as she put some avocado fries on her plate, next to a heaping mound of poke salad. "If she wasn't working right now, I'd get her on the phone so she could listen in. But since Kate works days and Jane works nights, I suppose she will have to get the CliffsNotes. Your mom and I have called you here tonight because we have news. I am officially retiring and handing over the reins of the Forsyth Galloway Inn to your mama."

It wasn't exactly a surprise, since Gigi had been talking about doing this for at least the past ten years, but it was a surprise that the official day had finally arrived.

"It's always a special day in our family's history when we hand off the property to the next generation. It propels our heritage. It keeps our legacy and the mission of my great-great-grandparents alive. That's why it's so important that you girls start preparing for the day when it will be your turn to take it over. Even though y'all grew up here and you have lives away from the inn right now, you'll need to start thinking of yourselves as Zelda's apprentices."

Elle glanced at her mother, who looked pale and unfocused. She watched Zelda throw back her drink, refill her glass and chug it.

"Are you okay, Mom?" Elle placed her hand on her mother's as she tried to reach for a third refill.

"No, I'm not okay. Not really. I'm happy for Gigi. She deserves to retire. You're almost eighty-five years old, for God's sake. You should've retired a long time ago.

The only reason you didn't was because I wasn't ready to take over and you were tied to this place."

"Zelda," Wiladean's voice was low and serious. "I thought we worked this out."

Zelda laughed, but there were tears in her eyes. "We did. Because there is no other answer. There is no choice. We were born into this godforsaken prison of an inn and all choice has been taken from us. I'm still not ready to take over, but if I don't take over for you after you retire, who will? Do we expect the girls to give up the lives they've made for themselves to jump in? I wouldn't foist this burden on anyone, much less my daughters."

Gigi looked bewildered. "What are you saying, Zelda?"

"What I'm saying, Mama, is I don't think I'll ever be ready to run this place." Zelda reached out and picked up the manila folder she'd brought in with her. She opened it and shook out a smattering of glossy brochures. They spilled out onto the table. "I'm saying that I don't want to be tied to this inn until I'm eighty-five years old. After Fred left, I quit living. I gave up on myself and the things in life that make me happy. I did that because I felt so damned guilty that I almost lost everything to a man who said he loved me and then tried to take our family for a ride.

"It was a pretty dumb thing to do—to give up on myself. I may be a little late to the party, but I need to invest in me for a while."

She picked up a brochure about a tour of the Machu Picchu area; another one was for the Galápagos Islands, and yet another one was for a three-week meditation cruise.

"I want to do these things," she said. "I want to travel and find myself again. But I won't be able to do that if my future is decided for me day in and day out right here at the Forsyth Galloway Inn. This place is a prison."

Gigi sat in her seat looking as if she'd been slapped in the face.

"What are you suggesting, Zelda? That we sell the place? That we throw six generations of history out like it was yesterday's garbage?"

Gigi didn't give Zelda a chance to answer. She got up and walked out of the room. Zelda and Gigi were prone to disagreeing, but they had never arrived at an impasse like this one.

Elle was at a loss for how she would fix this rift.

Chapter Nine

The next morning, Elle's phone rang as she was getting out of the shower. She wrapped herself in a towel and answered.

"Hello?"

"What's this I hear about you and Daniel Quindlin?"

It was her older sister, Jane. Elle realized with a sinking stomach that she should've called her after all that had transpired last night. It wasn't necessary though, because Kate had most likely called Jane on her way home, leaving a message if Jane had still been working. She could picture Kate saying, "Call me. Call me as soon as you get off work. I don't care how late it is." Because she was that eager to slide into the juicy gossip-palooza mud.

"Good morning, Jane. What exactly did you hear?"

"Don't be coy, Elle. Kate said you're in love with Daniel Quindlin. Do I need to come down there and hold an intervention?"

Her stomach twisted. She wished she could rewind and take back the words, because they were premature. Once they'd fallen out of her mouth, like a wad of gum she shouldn't have been chewing, she had regretted them. Regretted them to the point that all night she'd kept waking up, hearing herself saying *I think I'm falling in love with Daniel Quindlin.*

She didn't know what she wanted. Because she didn't want to stop seeing him. But the big fat L-word made her feel like she'd jumped out of the open door of an airplane without a parachute and was free-falling toward a hard impact.

Her head was spinning, and she didn't want to have this conversation with Jane right now.

"If it will make you come home, sure, knock yourself out, come hold an intervention."

"But Daniel Quindlin, Elle? What kind of an alternate universe did I wake up in this morning?"

Elle seized the opportunity to change the subject. "Speaking of, what are you doing up this early? You've only had about four hours of sleep."

"I'm calling to see if you've lost your mind. *Daniel Quindlin?* What the hell?"

She said his name like he was garbage and even though she knew her big sister thought she had her best interest at heart, it irked her.

"No, my mind is right where I left it." She pulled the phone away to check the time. It was just before 7:00. Daniel and Chloe were due to arrive at 8:00; she still

had to dry her hair and she could use a cup of coffee—
or two. "Could you please hear me out before you jump
to conclusions?"

Jane was quiet, but Elle could virtually hear her mind
trying to reconcile the details of the conversation she'd
overheard before the wedding with a plausible explanation of how Elle could even stand to be in the same
room with Daniel, much less entertain romantic notions.

For the second time in as many days, she heard herself telling the story of seeing Daniel jogging in the
park and him showing up at the inn.

"I suppose Kate told you that Mom and Gigi hired
him to fix the old hurricane damage as well as do some
renovations?"

"Yeah, apparently you've all had a drink of the Daniel Kool-Aid."

"Before you crucify them, you need to hear the facts.
Look, the bottom line is what happened between Roger
and me really isn't Daniel's fault. I appreciate you cir-
cling the wagons, but Roger cheated on me. Apparently,
it had been going on for a while—like the whole time
we were apart in college and even as recent as the night
before the wedding. I didn't want to hear the gory details, but I'm guessing that it was bad enough for Daniel to nudge Roger, and Roger—whether it was in a
moment of conscience or he was just being true to his
cowardly ways—ran. Daniel didn't kidnap him. Roger
ran. Jane, as humiliating as it was to be left at the altar,
I believe Daniel saved me from a really bad marriage."

"So, is this like a delayed offshoot of Stockholm syn-
drome?" Jane's tone softened, but it still held notes of

confusion. The answer had Elle's mind winging back to that day in the library when Daniel had kissed her.

"I'm going to tell you something I've never told anyone before. I'm telling you this in the cone of silence. So, you can't tell anyone." She started to say, *Not that it matters.* But it *did* matter. It mattered to her.

"Daniel kissed me when we were in high school, when I was tutoring him. He had only lived here about a month. I was dating Roger at the time, but it was before he and Roger had become friends. He kissed me, and I was so sheltered and naive he scared me to death. Jane, he made me feel things I'd never felt before. Even though we mostly avoided each other after it happened, I guess I never really got over that kiss. I didn't even know it until I saw him again. It made me a believer in that old saying, 'There's a thin line between love and hate.' It's so complicated, but I think I have a better idea of which side of that line I'm standing on now. Because I certainly don't hate him anymore."

Jane was silent. Elle's heart sank. She wasn't sure what she'd wanted Jane to say, but she only knew that confession made her feel vulnerable because she didn't want her to downplay it or say, *So...?* That kiss had shaped her, even if it had taken all these years to realize it. Maybe she hadn't been ready for Daniel Quindlin back then. Maybe she still wasn't ready for him. But the only way she'd ever know if she was edging too close to the fire was to risk getting burned.

Chloe was a stabilizer. Everyone minded their manners when she was at the inn. Everyone—especially Zelda and Gigi, bless their hearts—made an effort to watch their tones and soften their prickly edges. Because despite the tragedy of her daddy being in the hospital, Chloe was still a happy little girl with a sweet disposition. When she was around, she brightened the Forsyth like Savannah sunshine on a perfect spring day.

Plus, the guests loved her and the ever-present Princess Sweetie Pie, who was always tucked under Chloe's arm or sitting close by when she was playing the My Little Pony game or painting at the small easel that Elle and Daniel had picked out for her. Gigi told Chloe she was the ambassador of the Forsyth Galloway Inn.

"It's like you're a princess who makes everyone feel happy and welcome." That was the beginning of a brand-new game of make-believe that had Chloe pretending to be a princess. Gigi was her faithful servant.

They were having so much fun that it shouldn't have been surprising when Gigi suggested Daniel and Elle have a date night so that Chloe could stay and play longer. After what had transpired the other night when she had blurted out her feelings for Daniel and then Gigi and Zelda had come to verbal blows, Elle had been hesitant to ask for Chloe to stay, but Gigi had relieved her of that task by volunteering. Actually, she had insisted.

On Friday morning, when Daniel and Chloe had arrived, Gigi said, "Why don't you leave that sweet little girl here with me and y'all go out and have a good time. She goes off to camp next week. I'm going to miss having her here."

That evening, he had done just that. He had gone home to change and then returned to the Forsyth to pick up Elle.

* * *

She was gorgeous in the not-too-dressy black dress—that still showed she'd made an extra effort—and flat sandals laced around her tan ankles. She looked so good it almost stopped him in his tracks. She had twisted her long, blond hair off her face and put on enough makeup to look polished but not spackled.

First they drove to the Crystal Beer Parlor on Jones Street, where they had dinner and drinks. They were seated side by side in a booth in the back of the restaurant. He'd turned on the seat so that he was facing her. His knee was touching her thigh under the checkered tablecloth. He put his hand on her leg, caressing it, inching it ever so slightly under the hem of her dress.

"What's the story behind this place?" Her body shifted so that she pressed into him a little more. The connection was electric. He could tell that she felt it, too. He wished he could scoop her up and take her to his house and forget the pretense of dinner. But he wanted to give her more than that. Their history had been him taking what he wanted. He wanted to show her that he was better than that. She deserved better than that.

"It's funny, I've been here more times than I can count," she said, "but I don't know the Crystal's history. All I know is it has my favorite burger in the world. I'd bet money that you know all about this place, don't you?"

He nodded. "For about thirty years, this place used to be a grocery store. The Gerken Family Grocery Store opened back in the early 1900s. In the early 1930s, they sold the place to Blocko Manning and his wife, Connie. The Crystal was one of the first places to serve alcohol after the repeal of Prohibition. It's rumored that Manning ran a little hooch back in the day and may have even operated a speakeasy."

"Right here?" Elle asked.

"The speakeasy was in the basement. The house of ill repute was upstairs."

"If these walls could talk."

"A lot of people would've gotten into trouble."

"You're really passionate about knowing all this history, aren't you?"

He nodded. "If you look deep enough, you see that everyone has a story. I think it's fascinating. I love collecting deeper stories about Savannah."

"Tell me another one," she said.

He thought for a moment. "Okay, here's one. Did you know Savannah has more than one hundred distinct neighborhoods in six principal areas of the city?"

"And what are those principal areas?" She bit her bottom lip and he leaned in and kissed her, drawing her lip between his teeth, biting it and teasing it.

"Downtown, Midtown, Southside, Eastside, Westside and West Chatham." As he ticked off the locations, he scooted his finger higher up her thigh with each one.

She leaned in closer. "I like all this…history. Tell me more."

Her hand fell onto his thigh, dangerously close to his crotch. She let it linger, tracing small circles on the leg of his jeans. His body responded.

"The historic district encompasses about two and a half square miles and houses around twenty-three hundred buildings—give or take a few."

She was teasing him and it was driving him crazy.

"And what else?"

His hand was at the base of her panties, now. He could feel the lace. He trailed his finger along the edge of it. She shivered.

"The architecture is in a handful of different styles. Steamboat Gothic, which is way over the top, and Colonial, which is pretty straightforward. Federal architecture and Italianate style and, of course, Victorian." He slid his finger under the edge of the lace and she shuddered. "I know there are others...but I can't think of them right now."

Out of his peripheral vision he saw someone moving toward their table. Their server.

"To be continued," he whispered, as he discreetly withdrew his hand.

After dinner they drove back to Hall Street. Daniel parked the truck at the inn so they could get out and walk. It was unseasonably warm tonight, the perfect night to show Elle his favorite places in Savannah.

"I have a surprise," he said. He reached into the back seat and grabbed a small cooler. Inside was a bottle of champagne and a couple of red plastic cups.

"Care for a to-go cup to start off our champagne tour of the city? This is a classy operation."

To-go cups were one of the guilty pleasures of walking in the city. It was perfectly legal to take your beverage of choice for a stroll.

"This is perfect," she said. "Are you planning on getting me drunk so you can take advantage of me?"

"Would you like that?"

The question hung in the air between them.

She leaned in and kissed his neck, trailing her lips

up to his ear, where she whispered, "Yes. I would. But you wouldn't have to get me drunk. And you wouldn't be taking advantage of me."

Her breath was hot and sweet and he almost came undone as he pulled her in for a long, slow kiss. If not for the damned cooler in the well between them, he would've pulled her onto his lap and finished what they'd started in the Crystal.

But the blockade was a sign that he needed to slow things down. So, he poured the champagne into the two cups and handed her one. "Wait right here," he said. "I'm coming around to open your door."

As they walked up Whitaker toward Jones Street, it gave him a chance to cool off. "There are hundreds of houses and buildings worthy of me pointing out. But I've narrowed it down to my favorite dozen."

"Oh, yeah? I can't wait to see what you have planned."

He put his free hand on the small of her back. "You know the phrase 'keeping up with the Joneses,' right? They say it originated right here on Jones Street. They say it's supposed to be the most beautiful street in Savannah."

"I've heard that." She smiled as she narrowed her eyes at him. "Is it true?"

"Look around. What do you think?"

"It's pretty. In an understated way. Not grand and flashy like some of the mansions on the squares."

"Exactly. They say Jones Street doesn't house *attractions* as much as the street is an attraction in itself."

"I have to admit," Elle said looking around in wonder, "as much as I love the Forsyth and all that it means to our family, sometimes I wouldn't mind trading my portion for a cozy house of my own…some place like Jones Street."

"Even with the Forsyth right around the corner? Could you really live here knowing your family home was in someone else's hands?"

"Probably not. But you can't blame a girl for wanting a life of her own. That's what I was trying to build in Atlanta."

"Sometimes fate has its own plans for you," he said.

"That's what my mother is trying to come to terms with right now." She sipped her champagne. "Gigi has announced her retirement, but Mom isn't sure she wants her turn at running the inn. She seems to think fate is tempting her to travel."

They walked up Abercorn Street toward Lafayette Square.

"What does that mean for the inn? Can anyone else step in and help out?"

"We're trying to figure that out. We don't have other family. It's been a point of pride that the Forsyth Galloway Inn has always been run by the women on Gigi's side of the family. She had a sister, our aunt Gertie, but she never had children. She's gone now. It's all come down to us. Jane is in New York, Kate has built a career doing hair…

"I'm really bummed because of what transpired between Mom and Gigi. Gigi announced her plans to retire and Mom says she's going to the Galápagos and will talk about what's happening with the inn when she gets back. I don't know how long I will be here to help out."

His gut knotted. She was still talking about leaving. When it seemed like they were making progress, she wanted to go. But something told him to listen, not to interject.

"I can understand where both of them are coming from. You never had the pleasure of meeting my father, Fred.

"He and my mother divorced when my sisters and I were little. Not too long after that, Fred took my mom to court and tried to claim half the Forsyth as a marital asset."

"I'll bet Gigi didn't think much of that," Daniel said.

"No, she didn't. Neither did my mom. Fred ended up losing the case because the Forsyth was in Gigi's name. It cost my mom a whole lot of money and even more heartache. He really kind of wrecked her life. Ever since then, Mom has been pretty subdued. Sometimes it even seems like she's doubted her own judgment. Because of that she's been cautious. Suddenly, she's waking up and feeling like life has passed her by and she wants to make up for lost time. She says she's afraid running the inn will keep her from the life she wants to lead. She says the thought of being tied to the inn feels like a prison sentence. But, at the same time, she acknowledges that Gigi should be able to retire."

"You know, everything could be solved and everyone would be happy if you would move back and take over the Forsyth," he said.

Elle's eyes clouded. "Everyone but me. I wouldn't mind being back in Savannah, but I'm not sure I want to be tied down to the inn. It's a huge commitment."

He wondered if she was talking about relationships, too. Was she still closing herself off after what happened with Roger? A brush with something like that would make a person skittish, but it was almost masochistic to play it so safe that future relationships were cut off before they could even begin. He'd gone through something similar after losing his wife. When you love deeply, you open yourself up to potentially big hurt.

They walked in silence to the fountain in Lafayette Square. They could see the grand spires of the Cathedral of Saint John the Baptist glowing through the live oaks like twin apparitions. Elle stopped and pointed to them. "That's so beautiful." She shook her head. A resigned smile turned up the corners of her lips.

"I'm so sorry I was going on and on about my family like that, Daniel. I'll stop now. I am not going to ruin this fabulous night you set up by complaining about the most recent war my mother and Gigi have waged." She gestured, as if indicating a door. "This is the portion of the tour where Mom and Gigi exit and we continue."

She smiled up at him and he wanted to photograph her with his mind to remember exactly how she looked at that moment.

"I never knew you were so easy to talk to," she added.

He answered her with a kiss.

"You're absolutely right," she said. "When you look deeper, you see qualities you've never seen before."

They continued across the square and stood in front of the Andrew Low House, home of the father-in-law of Girl Scouts founder Juliette Gordon Low.

"The architecture of this place combines Grecian details with elements of the Italian villa style and has one of Savannah's most stunning ironwork balconies.

Back in the day, you could tell how wealthy a man was by how much ironwork he had outside his house. It was expensive and a great way to flaunt deep pockets."

As they walked, Daniel pointed out several more of his favorite spots, including the birthplace of Juliette Gordon Low and Flannery O'Connor, more for the history than the architecture.

"I've been to a lot of those places when I was a kid on school field trips," she said. "But it's kind of sad that you can live right in the midst of so much history and stop seeing it."

"I'm happy to reacquaint you," he said, taking her hand.

"As long as there won't be a pop quiz."

"Never. You know how I was when it came to school."

"That's only because they didn't tap into what moves you."

You move me.

"It doesn't matter that you didn't go to college. It isn't for everyone. You're more successful than many who did. Daniel, you're so smart and good at what you do."

"You know I was never really into school. My grades and attendance record were bad and I had a couple of brushes with the law. None of that did me any favors. After my grandmother's house burned, I left Savannah. I never graduated from Savannah Country Day. I ended up getting a GED."

"You always were more interested in working than in textbooks, weren't you?" she asked.

He nodded. "I used to skip school a lot so I could work. After my parents died and Aidan and I came to live with our grandmother, times were tight. Most of the contractors would pay me cash for day labor. They didn't care how old I was if I showed up on time and was willing and able to work. At the time, money won out over algebra and English lit."

"You were getting an education of a different type. Is that where you learned how to build houses?"

He nodded. "I learned the construction business and it ended up serving me pretty well."

"It sure did," she said as they stopped in front of the looming terracotta-colored Sorrel-Weed house.

She grimaced. "Tell me something good about this one."

"Why? What's wrong?"

"You know Sorrel-Weed is supposed to be one of the most haunted places in the country, if not the world, right? It was featured on a show about the most terrifying places in the Unites States."

"Yeah, want to take the ghost tour?" He gestured to the people queuing up to have the daylights scared out of them.

"No. Absolutely not. I don't do scary."

"You were born in Savannah and you don't do scary? You do know that the entire city is built over a graveyard, don't you?"

She put her hands over her ears. "Lalalalalalala! I can't hear you. I have never seen a ghost. I don't want to see a ghost. I believe in happy."

She shivered and crossed her arms in front of her.

"As in fairy tales and happily-ever-after?"

His stomach hitched, because for the first time in his life, he might let himself believe a happy ending was possible. Because he could totally see being happy ever after with her. Their gazes caught and something shifted between them.

"Tell me why you picked this one as one of your favorites."

He took a deep breath, reluctant to break the spell by talking about architecture. "This house is mostly done in the Greek Revival style, but it has English Regency influences and lots and lots of ghosts."

"Stop!" She made a face at him and pretended to swat him. When her hand brushed his arm, he pulled her in for a kiss. They stood there on the sidewalk lost in each other's embrace, and the rest of the world—the haunted house, the tourists who had to walk around them and all the fears and ghosts that had haunted him and made him so uncertain—faded away.

He had no idea how much time had passed when they finally broke apart, but he put his arm around her and they continued up Bull Street.

"Elle Clark?" a woman called to them from a streetside table at The Public on Bull Street. "Is that you?"

Daniel recognized Daisy Carter. They'd gone to high school with her at Savannah Country Day. He kept his arm around Elle, prepared for her to pull away, but she didn't.

They stopped and Daisy got up from her table. As she approached, she glanced at Daniel and her eyes flashed as if she'd uncovered the scoop of the century.

"Well, look at that," Daisy said. "It *is* you and look who you're with—Daniel Quindlin. Of all people. This is a surprise. It's like old home week. I haven't seen either of you since—"

The wedding. She didn't say it, but she didn't have to. He read it in the way her smile faltered then turned smug.

A wave of heat rushed through his body.

"Hi, Daisy." Elle said.

Daisy stepped forward to hug Elle.

"Are you back in Savannah now?" Daisy asked Elle as she eyed Daniel.

"I'm a teacher in Atlanta and I'm home for a visit during the holidays. What are you up to these days?"

"I married Lance Drayton three years ago. Do y'all remember him? He graduated three years ahead of us. We have two kids—a little girl named Annabelle and a boy. Our Chase is the oldest. I am absolutely loving life as a stay-at-home mom. Lance and I are having dinner with another couple." She gestured toward the table. "Would you like to join us? We can see if we can pull up two more chairs."

The table for four was cozy with the way the surrounding diners were packed in. It would've been tricky to wedge in two more chairs. Plus, it was clear that they were nearing the end of their meal. Daniel wondered if Daisy was simply unaware or if it was an empty offer because she hadn't liked him in high school. He and Aidan were scholarship kids at a school with mostly rich kids. He was pretty sure her feelings hadn't changed. It wasn't the first time he'd seen her around town. It was, however, the first time she'd spoken to him. The rebel in him wanted to call her bluff and agree to join them, but why would he want to do that when he and Elle were having a great time on their own?

They politely declined and made the appropriate noises when Daisy said that the four of them should get together for dinner. It would never happen, despite Daisy's promise to give Elle a call soon so they could set up something.

"We obviously have a lot of catching up to do," Daisy said.

As they walked away, Daniel was relieved when Elle slid her hand into his, as if silently saying, "Let's give them something to talk about." After they were a safe distance away, he said, "I suppose it was bound to happen sometime."

"What?" Elle asked, sounding unfazed.

"That we would run into someone we knew." Someone from high school. Someone who had been at the wedding and witnessed him nudging Roger and Roger bolting, leaving Elle alone and mortified.

"Sure you don't want to go back and spend the rest of the night with Daisy and company?" he asked.

She made a face at him. "Thanks, but I'll pass. Ironic that we should run into her next to the granddaddy of all haunted houses."

"You said it, not me," he said.

"But you were thinking it."

He shrugged. "Yes, I was, and I'll try to be a better person and think nicer thoughts."

"You're such a good influence on me," she said.

He laughed. "My, how times have changed."

They walked for about ten minutes, up Bull Street to Wright Square and across York Street to Oglethorpe Square to the Owens-Thomas House.

"This is a cool place. Have you ever been inside?" he asked.

"Ages ago," she said. "It's been so long, I really don't remember it."

"We'll have to come back in the daytime and do the tour," he said. "This place has a lot of history. It's part of the Telfair now. So, it has a lot of authentic furnishings from the early nineteenth century. It's a perfect example of English Regency architecture.

"See the cast iron around the sides? The house is famous for being one of the first to have a cast iron side veranda and it's where the Revolutionary War hero, the Marquis de Lafayette, stayed. He stood right there on that veranda when he addressed the citizens of Savannah."

It was getting late. Daniel knew that there was a fine line between sharing his passion for Savannah architecture and making her eyes glaze over. So, they headed back to the inn. It was a pretty twenty-minute walk, made festive by the Christmas decorations. Time flew. It wasn't long enough.

That was when Daniel knew he was in trouble. When was the last time he'd spent the whole evening with a woman and didn't want the night to end—or he hadn't been planning his strategy to get her back to her place for a little fun and afterward he could leave on his terms?

It was the strangest feeling. His body craved her, but he didn't want to move too fast and mess things up. Plus, when they finally did take things to the next level, he didn't want to rush. He wanted to have the whole night. He wanted her face to be the last thing he saw when he closed his eyes and first thing he saw when he woke up the next morning. He wanted to bring her breakfast in bed and not have to worry about doing right by Chloe.

When they turned into Hall Street off Whitaker, she said, "Can you stay out here a little longer or do you need to go in and get Chloe?"

"You tell me." He pulled her hand up to his lips and kissed her knuckles. "Chloe's probably asleep by now, but I don't want to take advantage of your grandmother."

"Then how about taking advantage of me?"

She took him by the hand and led him to his truck. "Open the doors."

He loved the mischievous glint in her eyes. His body instantly responded. "Should we drive somewhere else?"

The truck was parked across the side street and down a few yards from the Forsyth.

"We're fine," she said.

"Won't they talk?"

"Let them talk. I'm sure Daisy is already burning up the party line. This will give everyone else something to talk about."

They got in, he put Ray LaMontagne on the stereo and they made out in his truck, lips and mouths and hands exploring every inch of each other that was physically possible to explore in the cabin of a pickup truck. The back seat was too small and there was the matter of the cooler, which he strongly considered tossing out the window, but that would've been a mood killer.

"I want you to make love to me, Daniel."

"I want that, too, but not here. Not like this."

He wasn't ready to say good-night, but he knew if they kept up what they were doing, he wasn't going to be able to control himself for much longer. He kissed her for a long, hot moment and then she slid back into the passenger seat, righting her underwear and dress as he buttoned his jeans and tried to convince his body that this was really the best way.

Damn liar.

Hell, he wanted her. But he wanted her naked and in his bed. He didn't want their first time to happen in a car.

As if reading his mind, Elle said, "I feel like we're back in high school."

"Yeah, but you and I never made out in a car."

"We didn't. We made out in the school library, remember?"

"I could never forget that."

She shifted in the seat and he pulled her to him so that her back was against his chest. He put his arms around her.

"We need to make up for lost time." Her voice was raspy.

His hand slid down to her bare arm and he traced small circles on her skin. The silky smoothness of it tempted him to finish what they'd started. Instead, he shifted, holding her in place against his chest with his left hand while he grabbed the champagne bottle with his right hand.

"Do you want another red cup?" he asked.

She shook her head and took the bottle from him and raised it to her lips.

"I thought you hated me after I kissed you in the library," he said.

"I was scared to death of you." She handed him the

bottle. He turned his head to the side and sipped. "You made me feel things I didn't want to feel."

"Do I still do that to you?" he asked.

"You still scare me. But now I'm ready for you. Before, I wasn't ready for you."

"I promise I won't hurt you, Elle."

"I know you won't. You're a better person than... others."

She'd almost said *Roger.*

Damn him. Somehow the specter of the jackass still managed to materialize and wedge itself between them. Even all these years later.

He can try, but I'll be damned if I'm going to let him.

"We definitely have some lost time to make up for. Chloe goes to camp next week. I'll find a way for us to have some time together."

Chapter Ten

Zelda was still downstairs sitting at the front desk with a mug of tea after Elle said good-night to Daniel and Chloe, even though the little girl had gone to bed shortly before 8:30 and they'd locked the Forsyth's front doors at 10:00, leaving the guests to let themselves in with an access code.

She looked up from the magazine she was thumbing through. "How was your date?"

"It was nice. We went to the Crystal Beer Parlor and then we mapped out an architecture walking tour that might work. Maybe we can try it out sometime soon?"

"That would be lovely." Zelda smiled, but it seemed forced and she looked pale and drawn.

"Do you feel like talking for a few minutes?" she asked. "I'll go fix you a cup of tea. There's still water in the kettle."

Elle knew from experience that this meant she had something on her mind. "I'm not tired. We can talk."

Zelda got to her feet and headed toward the kitchen and tried to make small talk. "Is that all y'all did? Walk around?"

Elizabeth flashed her a bewildered smile. "*Yes*. What else would we do?"

"Oh, Elle, don't be such a prude. You're twenty-eight years old. I'm sure you're not a blushing virgin. Your lips are swollen and you have a little bit of beard burn on your cheeks."

Yeah, but no matter how old I am, it's still awkward to discuss it with my mom.

Elle's hand flew to her lips and she cringed. "Mom, can we not? Please?"

"That's my clumsy way of saying I get it. Daniel is a sexy guy."

"Okay, I'm going to bed. Good night."

"No, Elizabeth," she said, stopping at the kitchen door. "Please stay and talk to me. I promise to keep it PG. I understand you wanting to move on after what happened with Roger. That was six years ago. Just because I had a bad experience with your dad, it doesn't mean I should project it onto you. I mean, you're young and vibrant. You should fall in love with whoever you want to love."

After Gigi's matchmaking and her mom's change of tune, falling in love with Daniel was beginning to feel like selection by committee and that felt a little weird. It seemed a little forced. Even so, Zelda's heart was in the right place, and clearly, there was more that she wanted to talk about. Elle followed her into the kitchen.

Zelda took a teabag from the tea chest and held it up. "Is chamomile okay?"

"That sounds good."

Elle had a distinct feeling that her mother hadn't waited up to discuss Daniel.

"What's on your mind, Mom?"

Zelda didn't answer as she focused on pouring hot water from the kettle into Elle's cup and then into her own to refresh it. She brought both mugs over to the table and sat down across from Elle, in their respective let's-have-a-talk places.

"I've been doing a lot of thinking," she said, staring down into her cup. She paused, silence heavy between them, but Elle resisted filling the void.

"I'm a little ashamed of myself for the fit I threw the other night when Kate was over."

"Mom, it's okay. It's not an easy situation. I'm still trying to figure out if this place is a gift or a yoke. But it is our legacy. We are so very fortunate to have it."

"That's exactly why I came to the conclusion that I did," Zelda said. "I will take my turn running the Forsyth. It wouldn't be fair to you three girls or Gigi if I skipped out and shirked my responsibility. Gigi has worked long past what she should've and that was because of me. I suppose I should've spoken up and urged her to retire sooner, but I didn't want to take over." She sighed. "I suppose Machu Picchu and the Galápagos and Greece will wait for me." She laughed. "They've waited this long. What's another twenty years?"

Her eyes looked sad. The truth shone through. It wasn't what she wanted. Elle didn't know what to say.

Zelda wasn't the type to play the false martyr and expect her to jump in and relieve her of the burden.

"I keep hearing Gigi say, *What do you want me to do? Sell the place?*" Zelda had tears in her eyes. "She's right. There really isn't another solution. We can't afford to hire a manager. It's up to me now, and I'm certainly not going to be the one who gives up on a six-generation legacy."

"I'll help you for as long as I can," Elle said. The unspoken part was, *Until the county calls and tells me they have another teaching job for me.*

Zelda nodded and a single tear meandered down her cheek.

But what if they didn't have another job for her? Budget cuts for the school year had been deep.

Elle used a spoon to take the tea bag out of her cup and wound the string around the bag and spoon to squeeze out the excess water. She bit her bottom lip against the phantom feel of Daniel's lips on hers, against the memory of his hands on her breasts, pushing under her dress. God, she wanted him; it was a need that consumed her more than she could process.

"What do you think about this?" she said as she set down the spoon. "Why don't we leave it up to fate? If the county calls after the first of the year with another job for me, it means I'll go to Atlanta. If they don't, I'll put off the job search and move back to Savannah and help you run the Forsyth."

Zelda gasped. Her hand flew up to her open mouth and the tears she'd been holding back spilled out onto her cheeks.

"Would you really do that for me?"

Elle nodded. "I would."

For you. And for Daniel. Though she wasn't sure she would mention this wager with the heavens to him.

When Daniel arrived at the Forsyth on Monday, Elle was in the sunroom working in her art journal and tending to the guests. Because of the construction, they'd closed the dining room and moved the guests' breakfast into the sunroom.

Monday was generally a slower day. To compound matters, when they had let some of their bookings know that there would be construction happening at the inn, the guests had canceled. So, today was even slower than usual. Since Elle had volunteered to tend the breakfast, she'd brought along her art journal, figuring it would be a good time to reconnect with it.

In Atlanta, she'd been so busy with school—lesson plans and trying out new techniques that were appropriate for elementary school age kids—that she hadn't allowed herself to indulge in much personal creativity. Now she used matte gel medium to glue down some collage elements that she had collected—a paper luggage tag she'd found in the hallway, a coaster from the Crystal she'd picked up the night of her date with Daniel, a receipt from her purse, a feather she'd found in the park across the street and the tab from the end of a tea bag string.

After the matte medium dried, she would paint and draw over the items and add additional layers of collage ephemera. But first she would have to wait for everything to set. It was an exercise in patience as well as creative expression. She'd forgotten how nice it was to exercise her creative muscles.

She also had an ulterior motive for bringing out the journal. She wanted to see if there was any spontaneous interest from the guests. The way she would gauge it would be by seeing if anyone came over and either asked what she was doing or simply watched as she worked.

Seven people had come down for breakfast and six of the seven had expressed an interest. Of the six, five had said they would be interested in taking a free art journaling workshop.

Five would be a nice number for a beginner class.

Without even asking Gigi or her mother, she made the executive decision to offer the Forsyth Galloway Inn's inaugural art class on Wednesday. She told her prospective students that all they would need was a journal or a notebook—the size, shape and type was up to them. If they wanted one like hers, they could find it at the SCAD bookstore on Martin Luther King Jr. Blvd. She would provide the rest of the materials.

She had glued down the last item into her own journal when she looked up and saw Daniel standing in the doorway. Happiness flooded through her at the sight of him standing there, all freshly showered and looking delicious.

"Good morning," she said.

"Good morning." He walked over and bent down to look at her open journal.

"How did Chloe do this morning when you dropped her off for her first day of camp?"

"She did great. She has a lot of friends doing the

camp. She was happy to see them. She waved goodbye to me and ran inside with them like a big girl. What's this?" He gestured to her open art journal.

"It's the first draft of my inaugural art class here at the inn. I'm glad to hear she was ready to have fun. We're going to miss her around here."

He gestured at the journal. "Does that make you the first artist in residence?"

"I guess it does. Or maybe art teacher in residence."

"Artist," he said. "Don't sell yourself short."

Elle shrugged against the thrill that coursed through her at his encouragement. It had been so long—since art school—since she'd thought of herself as an artist rather than an art teacher. There was safety in hiding behind the teacher label. As a teacher, she taught. Students looked up to her, counting on her expertise. There was rarely any judgment from the beginners she taught. Especially not among her elementary students. Tempera paint and modeling clay rarely brought out the kids' inner critic, except when she tried to sneak in a lesson about color theory or the different styles of the masters. And those were usually groans of constructive learning tainting a good old free-for-all with paint and brush. The kids didn't care if it was in the style of Jackson Pollock. All they knew was that it was fun to fling paint off a brush onto paper—and each other. Mostly onto each other.

Daniel carried over a chair that one of the guests had moved to another table and sat next to her. He ran a calloused thumb down the fan of completed pages in the front of the journal. "May I look? I just realized I haven't seen your art since high school."

Her first reaction was to hide her work, to protect herself. How long had it been since she'd laid herself bare in the form of her art?

"Careful." But she had been eager to render herself naked and vulnerable at his hands on Friday night when they'd made out in his truck. The memory of that night sent electric currents of longing pulsing through her and pooling in her center. "The matte medium I used to glue down the ephemera isn't dry yet."

However, it was set enough to hold. And if she could trust her fragile heart in his strong, capable hands, she could trust him with the various studies that had been closed off in this book, hidden away from critical eyes for years.

A million thoughts went through her head at the same time—Roger. Hurt. Love. Devastation. Vulnerability. Jilted. Nudged. Innocent. Wronged. Cheater. Naked. Hungry. Saved from making the worst mistake of her entire life.

"I'll be careful," he promised, and she let him slide the book closer to himself.

Elle held her breath as, with one hand, he carefully held out the page she had been working on when he'd entered the sunroom and thumbed through the rest with his free hand.

He was perfectly silent as he perused. Elle felt exposed and vulnerable, and she looked away and held her breath.

When a good five minutes had gone by and he hadn't said anything, but was still carefully flipping through the pages—maybe for a second or third time—she said, "They're just studies."

As if that made them illegitimate or somehow let her off the hook, released her from the liability and labels that might be slapped on from the opinions he was silently forming his head.

She wished he would say something. And then she hoped he wouldn't, as a sinking, drowning feeling made her wish she had never brought out her journal, inviting opinions.

But then a funny thing happened. The negative self-talk receded, and it was replaced by a soft voice that reminded her that she didn't need validation to be whole, to be an artist. A love of art was a gift and the gift she'd been given was hers. No one could take that away from her.

"These are great," he said, a note of wonderment coloring his voice. "Really great. Have you done any canvases since school? Wait, was that your work that was hanging in the dining room before we started the renovation?"

She suddenly remembered it was her work that he was talking about. Someone, probably Gigi or her mother, had taken the canvases down before the renovation had started so that they wouldn't get damaged.

"Yes, that's my work. It's from when I was in school at SCAD."

"Elle, why aren't you painting more? You are so talented. I always remembered that in high school you were so artistic, so well-rounded."

The thought of going into the speech about teaching being a time and inspiration suck and the whole ugly reality of needing to make a living so she could support herself…and Roger stealing her joy and maybe even a little bit—okay, a whole lot—of her self-confidence when he'd left her seemed exhausting. They were excuses.

So much had changed in the years since then. She already knew it was time to stop wallowing and start using her God-given gifts, even if she had to start with giving classes on art journaling to the guests who stayed at her family's inn. She'd still have time to paint.

That was the least she could do while she waited for word to come down about a teaching job.

"I have a surprise for you," Daniel said. There was a light in his brown eyes that hinted that she was going to like what he had to say.

"Chloe's friend Emma's mom asked if Chloe could go home with Emma after camp the day after tomorrow and have a sleepover. If you're free Wednesday night, come over and I'll fix dinner for you."

"How did the inaugural Forsyth Galloway Inn art class go?" he asked as he handed her a glass of Malbec on Wednesday evening.

It was the first time she'd been to his house. Actually, it was the first time in a while he'd spent any time there. He hadn't even put up any Christmas decorations. Since Aidan was still in the hospital and Daniel had been staying with Chloe at Aidan's house in the Habersham Woods area, his own house off Skidaway Road wasn't exactly convenient for dropping in or swinging by with Chloe in tow.

After Elle had agreed to have dinner with him, he'd gone by the hospital to check on Aidan—who was still improving, but not quite enough for them to ease up on the Propofol that was keeping him in deep sleep. Then he'd gone to the grocery store to pick up a couple of filets and lobster tails. He wasn't a chef by any means, but he did have his easy go-to meals. This was about as easy as they went, because he had no intention of spending the evening in the kitchen.

This was their first night alone: wherever it led, he wanted to spend as much time as possible with her.

"The class was a lot of fun, actually," she said. "Everyone who signed up—all five of them—" she laughed and rolled her eyes, as if the whole thing was no big deal "—showed up and they all seemed genuinely interested."

He touched his glass to hers. "That's fantastic. Do you think this could be an ongoing thing?"

She shrugged. "I don't know, we'll see. I forgot to tell you that my mom has had a change of heart. For the time being, she has agreed to take her turn running the inn. She's not happy about it, but she realized it's the right thing to do."

His stomach sank and he turned his attention to the asparagus spears he'd washed and set on the cutting board so she wouldn't see his disappointment. "So, this lets you off the hook, then?"

He glanced up to gauge her reaction. She was chewing on her bottom lip, looking contemplative.

"I don't know," she finally said. "We will have to see what happens."

He had to remind himself that this thing between them had only been going on for two weeks. Sometimes it seemed as if they had been together forever, when in reality they weren't *together*, but what was *together*?

Was it more than spending time together, seeing each other every day? Did they have to spell out that they were a couple? He wasn't good at this because he didn't know how to do this. All he knew was that now that she was in his life, he didn't want to lose her.

It was on the tip of his tongue to ask her what would happen to them if she did get another position in Atlanta and moved back, but he didn't want to pressure her. He didn't want to seem needy and vulnerable. He thought about how many times he had been on the other side of this situation and a woman that he'd liked well enough had expedited the end by initiating the "where do we stand, where are we going" conversation.

So, he let it drop because he didn't want to spoil their time together. He chopped and grilled and she asked about Aidan as she set the table. She hadn't been able to go to the hospital with him today because of the art class.

It dawned on him that this was the first time that he'd been in a hospital and hadn't been on the verge of a panic attack.

He filled her in and said Aidan's medical team was going to meet tomorrow and evaluate whether it was time to discontinue the Propofol.

Her mouth fell open and her blue eyes were huge and hopeful. "Should we be there? I'll go with you. Chloe will be so happy. We will finally be able to give her some good news. She might get to see her dad soon."

She genuinely cared about his family and what happened to them. She seemed emotionally invested in them. How could she not be emotionally invested in the two of them?

They stared at each other as the truth dawned clear and unmistakable. When they let down their guards, intimacy came so naturally. A closeness that was so profound and powerful it was all-consuming.

They'd trusted each other with their most intimate secrets. They knew the best and the worst of each other. Even though it scared him to think of caring for someone so deeply, he couldn't not care for her. This was Elizabeth—Elle. He'd already passed the point of no return. He'd be lying to himself if he didn't own up to the truth. He'd fallen for her. And hard.

The only question was, where did they go from here?

He knew what he wanted, but she still wasn't sure what she was going to do. He didn't want to pressure her.

So, now what?

But he swallowed the question and enjoyed her company and the delicious meal and the chocolate mousse he'd purchased for them to have for dessert. And focused on the positive when they moved into the living room and talking turned into touching, which morphed into kissing.

He responded by wrapping his arms around her and pulling her in close to his body as if he'd never let her go.

"I have a surprise for you," he said. "Wait here."

He went into his bedroom and returned with the small, rectangular package he'd gift wrapped himself in Christmas paper.

He handed it to Elle.

"What's this?" she asked.

"Your Christmas present. I thought you could use it now."

"Daniel, you didn't have to get me anything."

"I wanted to get it for you. When I saw it, I couldn't not get it for you. Open it."

He sat down next to her and she leaned in and kissed him.

He smiled. "You haven't even seen what it is."

She pulled the paper away, revealing an antique box which was designed to hold her brushes.

She gasped. "I love it, Daniel. Thank you."

When she opened the wooden box, there was another, smaller box inside.

"Daniel?"

"Open it," he urged.

She opened the small, square box and found a gold necklace with a tiny gold paintbrush charm.

"Oh! It's beautiful," she said.

"Let me put it on you." He took the necklace from her. She held her hair off her neck as he secured the clasp. When the fine chain fell into place, she reached up and fingered the little gold brush.

"Wear this and always remember who you are," Daniel said. "You're talented, Elle. Never forget that. And please never let those talents go to waste."

She leaned in and kissed him.

Every inch of her body was pressed against his. He lost himself in the heated tenderness of that kiss.

She tasted like chocolate and sunshine and the very meaning of love. He'd waited so long for her.

There was no hesitation in her kiss. This was a woman who knew exactly what she wanted—at least right now. The way her hands explored his body—his shoulders, his back, his waist—running her fingertips under the edge of the waistband of his jeans until she found where his shirttail ended and his bare skin began.

The feel of her hands on his lower back made him instantly hard. Her touch promised that she'd love him with a hunger that would knock him out and render him even more defenseless than he was now. It made him desperate to show her how much he ached for her, how he'd longed for this moment since the day he'd laid eyes on her in the library. Rather than using words—because words could ruin everything right now—he conveyed his feelings with a deep kiss, claiming her lips in a way that was intended to sear her soul.

His need for her grew hot as fire as he held her and tasted her. He loved the feel of her curves, supple to his touch. He dropped his hands to her hips and pulled her onto his lap, on top of the evidence of his desire.

"I want you," she murmured breathlessly. "I want you now."

He raised his hands to her breasts, cupping them, memorizing her curves before teasing her hard nipples through her cotton blouse. She gasped. Her head dropped back and she seemed to lose herself in his touch.

Then it was his turn. She slid her hand between them and claimed the proof of his need for her, teasing him over and over, rubbing and stroking his desire through the layers of his jeans and briefs.

The sensation was almost too much to bear. It would've been even better if they could've gotten rid of the barriers between them.

He pulled her closer, leaning in to kiss the side of her neck, searing a path from the tender spot behind her ear, back to her full lips.

They were going to make love tonight. A shudder of pleasure racked his body. Suddenly he needed her naked so that he could bury himself inside her.

As if reading his mind, she said, "Let's go into the bedroom."

She took his hand and led him down the hall. When they were inside the doorway, he kissed her deeply—tongues thrusting, hands exploring, teeth nipping—as he walked her backward to the bed in a sensual dance. He wasn't cognizant of space and time. Only aware of tugging her shirt over her head, then slipping her bra straps off her shoulders, pulling the lacy fabric away so that her breasts were naked in his hands. When he took a nipple into his mouth, she moaned and need coursed through him hot and heady.

She unbuckled his belt and then the button on his jeans. Her fingers worked his zipper and she pushed his pants and underwear to the floor in one swift move. He stepped out of both and shrugged off his shirt.

Wanting to permanently imprint her on his senses, he deliberately slowed down, taking a moment to commit to memory the way her beautiful body felt under his hands.

He went back to finish ridding her of her bra, unhooking the front clasp and letting it fall away. He lowered his head and, in turn, took each breast into his mouth, sucking them until she cried out in pleasure. Then, when he was sure she was ready, he tugged down her pants and panties.

How long had he waited for this moment? It was definitely worth the wait. She was worth the wait.

She was so hot, they were going to be so good together he was surprised they didn't spontaneously combust. It was the feel of her in his hands—the touch of her soft, smooth skin under his work-roughened fingers—that was his touchstone.

One minute they were standing together naked, all the barriers between them gone, and the next they were a tangle of arms and legs. Then he lay her down on the bed and covered her body with his. She arched under him, demanding more. As if they were suspended in time, the world seemed to fade away. Exploring her body with his mouth and hands, he kissed and teased and tormented her, taking her to the brink of places she hadn't visited in a long time.

"Wait…" he said. "I need to get something."

He reached into the nightstand drawer and took out a foil packet.

She helped him put it in place.

"Now," she demanded, because if he made her wait another second, she might drown in her desire, greedy for the feel of him, wanting every masculine inch of him to cover her, to weigh her down, to be inside of her and make her body thrum with the pleasure of him inside her.

He lowered himself between her legs and found his way to her opening. He thrust his hips forward and with one bold stroke entered her.

She gasped from the sheer pleasure of finally feeling him inside her.

"Are you okay?" he asked.

"I've never been better," she whispered, barely able to get the words out.

His breathing rasped against her temple. He pulled out and then thrust a little deeper.

Her body clung to him, sliding, grabbing, pulsing and releasing over and over until waves of pleasure with weight and force crashed inside her.

They moved together as one. She was lost in the sheer ecstasy of their closeness. Until she couldn't hang on anymore. She let go and he helped her fall over the edge of pleasure.

His breath was hot and labored against her cheek. He began to move faster and faster, with a steady rhythm, until he gave a final thrust. A long, anguished groan sounded in his throat. He collapsed on top of her, kissing her tenderly, possessively. She reveled in their spent pleasure, in the feel of how his broad back narrowed at the waist, at the sheer masculine width and breadth of him. Until he pulled back a little, his lips still brushing hers.

"I love you, Elle," he whispered. "Let's get married."

What? She froze, wondering if she'd heard him right. Surely she hadn't heard him right? But when she pulled back and saw his earnest, unwavering gaze, she knew she'd heard him exactly right.

But she couldn't...

No.

Why did he say that? Why was he ruining everything?

Stop. This was too fast.

But you've been in love with this man since you were seventeen years old.

Loving someone from afar, someone you thought you could never have, was something altogether different from marrying him.

She'd been down that road once and it hadn't turned out well.

She'd sworn she wouldn't go there again.

I promise I won't hurt you, Elle.

His words echoed in her heart, swam in her head.

I know you won't. You're a better person than—

He's not Roger.

She knew he wouldn't hurt her, not on purpose. Then why was she so scared?

For a moment she was paralyzed. She wanted to pull away, but she couldn't move. She wanted to answer him, tell him to slow down, to not ruin things, but she couldn't even feel her face.

He must've felt her body stiffen, because every muscle in her body had tensed after he'd uttered those three words: *Let's get married.*

He raked a hand through his hair.

"Talk about words spoken in the heat of the moment that you'll regret in the morning." She tried to keep her voice light. She wanted to give him a chance to recover, because she was sure he hadn't meant it. The only way to save this was for him to pretend like he hadn't meant it.

Some men cried out a woman's name in the heat of passion, Daniel proposed.

Eh, better not say that.

She was searching for a way to lighten the moment,

but that probably sounded funnier in her head than it would hanging in the air between them.

But she needed to do something because she already knew this time she was going to be the one who ran.

Chapter Eleven

That man knew how to tie her belly up in knots. He wasn't even here and he was doing a number on her.

She should've known better. She should've put on the brakes before everything had skidded too close to the guardrail and spiraled out of control.

She stayed the night because by that time, it was late—about 3:00 a.m.—and she was too paralyzed to make the drive from Skidaway Road to downtown. There was always the chance that he would wake up and slap himself up the side of the head and say, *You're right. I got caught up in the heat of the moment. Let's scratch that from the records.*

Yeah, as if it was in Daniel's character to slap himself up the side of the head.

Hardly.

She hadn't wanted to run, but he had asked her to marry him.

Marry him!

Of course, after he'd said it and she had made the quip about words spoken in the heat of the moment that he would regret in the morning, he had gone silent. It would've been so much better if he'd said something—

I'm only kidding.

I'm serious, but take your time.

Anything!

Instead, he had reverted into the sullen, silent Daniel that she'd feared all those years ago. Only this time, she didn't fear that he would hurt her. On the contrary, it was her glib retort that had injured him gravely.

She wasn't sure if she hated herself more for that or because his words had rendered her so numb.

Why? Why had he ruined the otherwise good thing that they had going on?

Her heart twisted. The perverse thing was she didn't want to lose him. But she wasn't ready to commit. She didn't even know what tomorrow held, much less if she ever wanted to spend the rest of her life with somebody.

The next morning, he brought her a cup of coffee in bed.

"Do you need some time to think about things?" he asked.

"Things?" The word was so vague she wasn't sure if *things* meant the two of them or the proposal. Was it a proposal?

"I meant what I said. I want to marry you, Elle."

Yes, it was a proposal.

Oh, no.

"Daniel." She was still naked in his bed. She was covered by the sheets and had her knees pulled up to her chest, trying to make herself as small as possible, willing herself to disappear.

She didn't want to marry anyone. But he wasn't just anyone. She didn't know.

"Daniel, I have to be honest with you. The thought of getting married, of putting on another big white dress and walking down the aisle with all eyes on me makes me want to hyperventilate."

She could feel the gold necklace between her breasts. His hand was on her arm. And of all the ridiculous things, she liked it there. She craved his touch. It was soothing. It was a touchstone, but somehow, she still managed to short-circuit when her focus strayed from that isolated feeling. Because there it was—*marriage*. It made her mouth dry and her palms sweaty. It made her head swim and her heart hammer in her chest.

"It doesn't have to be a big to-do. It can be us and your family."

She tried to take in a deep breath, but there didn't seem to be enough oxygen in the room to fill her lungs.

"We can wait until Aidan is out of the hospital," he said, but the blood was rushing so loudly in her ears that she barely heard him add, "Chloe could be the flower girl."

When she didn't answer, he said, "We don't have to do it right now. We can wait."

It was the implied *BUT* at the end of the sentence that sent her over the edge.

BUT I need for you to commit now. BUT I need for you to assure me you won't run. BUT I need for you to promise me you'll move back to Savannah... And that meant she was putting herself at the mercy of someone else, putting her heart in his hands and trusting he wouldn't break it. Daniel had all but admitted she was the one he hadn't been able to forget because she was the one who'd remained out of his reach; she'd been unavailable.

What would happen once she'd agreed to be his? Once the chase was over and he'd caught her?

"I can't. I need to go." It was almost an out-of-body experience, as if she was floating above them looking down and seeing herself shove the coffee mug into his hand as she pushed away the top sheet and climbed out of bed.

His crew was at the inn working, but when it got to be 10:00 a.m. and he hadn't appeared, she texted him.

What time is the meeting about Aidan? I would like to go with you.

She held her breath waiting for his reply. Because the chance of him not replying made her heart ache so bad it felt like it would break into a million tiny pieces. She was such a freak. She didn't want to lose him, but she didn't want to marry him. At least not right now.

Enough time had passed that she thought he might not reply, or at least not immediately—and it made her unspeakably sad—but then his answer appeared on the screen.

1 p.m.

* * *

If Daniel could've kicked himself, he would've. What happened to playing it cool, not pressuring her, letting things unfold naturally?

All he knew was that one minute he was flying at the highest of highs and the next minute he was asking her to marry him.

And then he was crashing and burning.

There was no going back now. He thought it was all lost until she texted, wanting to go with him when he went to talk to the doctors about Aidan. Even then, he'd almost said no, or nothing at all, which essentially would have conveyed no, but the thought of going to that meeting and getting news—good or bad—without her was more than he could bear.

What was important now was Aidan. That was where his focus would be, but it would be good to have her with him.

As he was getting into his car to go to the meeting, the doctor called and asked him to meet him at the ICU nurses' station rather than his office as they'd originally planned.

He texted the change of venue to Elle.

True to her word, she was at the nurses' station at 1:00 p.m.

"Are you okay?" she asked when she saw him.

He gave a quick nod.

"Good." That was all that they said that could remotely pertain to what had happened the night before. Because right now the focus was on Aidan.

Standing there waiting for the doctor, who was not on time, to appear and deliver whatever news he had to give, Daniel suddenly realized the doctor might not necessarily be imparting good news. Each day, Aidan had been progressing well. The swelling had been receding and the tests seemed to be supporting the evaluation that he was moving in the right direction.

But as Daniel stood there looking at this woman he loved, this woman whose feelings didn't run quite as deeply for him as his did for her, he worried that maybe the bottom was about to really drop out of his life. Again.

Hospitals had never been the place of good news—not when his parents had been in the crash, not after his grandmother had the stroke, Not after Lana's aneurysm …

He was about to tell Elle that she didn't have to stay, when the doctor finally appeared, "Mr. Quindlin, I'm sorry I'm late. I was tied up with another patient. Please follow me, there's something I want you to see."

"Is everything okay? Is Aidan okay?"

The doctor didn't respond. He simply motioned for Daniel to follow.

"I'll wait right here," Elle said.

He nodded and walked behind the doctor. Even though it was the wrong time to think it—to think about anything besides his brother's well-being and the tough decisions he might possibly have to make in the coming days—it dawned on him that Elle hadn't necessarily showed up because she'd had a change of heart. Or because she cared for him any more deeply than a decent person cared for another who was experiencing hard times. Just as she'd gone from pissed-off and dismissive to kind and empathetic on the day of Aidan's accident, she very well could've been putting differences aside on what might be a day of devastating decisions, proving she was a good girl through and through.

The doctor stopped in front of Aidan's door. "Wait right here for a moment."

It was the longest damn moment of his entire life, but finally the doctor opened the door and invited Daniel inside. The first thing he saw was that Aidan was awake and out of the coma.

Elle hadn't been allowed to see Aidan because they were keeping his visits short and limited to immediate family until he moved to the progressive care unit. But she was so glad she could be there for Daniel when he came out and shared the good news.

Since Daniel couldn't go back to see Aidan until the next day, Elle suggested that they celebrate with a cup of coffee at the Sentient Bean, since the coffee shop was so close to the inn.

Maybe it was because she felt as if they'd left a lot of things unsaid. Maybe it was because she'd been at the hospital to learn news about an accident victim who'd been in a coma and that was a sharp reminder of the brevity of life and how things can change on a dime. But as they sat in funky upholstered chairs near the storefront window that looked out over Forsyth Park, Elle found herself rethinking her earlier panic.

"I was talking to my mom the other day about whether or not I would return to Atlanta or move back to Savannah and I told her that I was going to let fate decide. If I'm supposed to be here, then I won't get the job. If I'm supposed to go, a job will come through."

It wasn't exactly a promise, but it wasn't a hard no.

Once, Daniel had thought fate would spit on him at every opportunity. But in the wake of Aidan's recovery and good prognosis, he was hopeful that his fortunes were looking up.

That was why he didn't bring up the proposal again. In fact, he gave Elle some space. Not the kind of space that said he was mad at her or that he was too cool to talk about feelings, but enough to let this thing—whatever it was—between them gel…or fall apart.

He loved her. He'd always loved her.

He'd also lived without her all these years. He wasn't going to let her go, but…if he had to count on fate keeping her here in Savannah, he had to prepare himself to lose her. He loved her, but he wasn't going to cling to her if her heart was in Atlanta, away from him and the life he'd fought hard to build for himself in Savannah.

"I went to see Aidan Quindlin in the hospital today," Kate said.

Ah, so there it was. She thought there had to be a reason for her sister's unusual midday visit.

Elle was busy setting up supplies for her fourth art journal class. Since the first one had been such a success, they had put word out to the community via the arts bulletin board and they had received such an overwhelming response that they'd formed four new sessions and started a waiting list.

"I'm thrilled that he's doing so well," Elle said. "How did your visit go?"

Kate got a funny look on her face. "Hasn't Daniel told you?"

"Told me what? Is Aidan okay?"

"Sort of," Kate said as she followed Elle's lead and helped her sister sort ephemera into groups on her side of the table. "Physically, he seems to be recovering well. However, he does seem to be having some memory problems."

Daniel hadn't mentioned it. The thought that he hadn't shared it with her made her feel a little strange. "What do you mean?"

"For one, he has no idea who I am."

"Well, it has been a while since your disastrous prom date. Maybe he's chosen to block that memory."

Kate didn't laugh or come back with an otherwise snide retort. "I'm serious. He didn't remember me. I told him we went to prom together, thinking that would jog his memory, and he smiled and told me he was sorry but he didn't remember and looked at me as if that night ended well."

"Uh-oh, did you enlighten him?"

"Are you kidding? Of course not. What was I supposed to say? Once upon a time, you had a crush on me and I let you take me to prom, but I left with another guy?"

"Well, he's bound to remember sooner or later. What will you do then—or was this a onetime visit?"

"No, I sort of volunteered to come by every day and help him shave and cut his hair when he needs it. His right hand is in a cast and I thought it was the least I could do."

"Are you feeling guilty over prom? Seriously, Kate? That was so many years ago."

She shrugged. "Well, it can't hurt to help him out while he needs someone. I mean you, Mom and Gigi have been looking after Chloe."

"That was fun. She's been at camp this week and I've missed her. That's her little easel over there."

Sadness tugged at Elle's insides as she wondered if she'd ever see the little girl again. Since Aidan had awakened from his coma, Daniel had been taking her to the hospital every evening after picking her up from camp. Then the two of them had gone home...or somewhere. Just not here.

Since their night together, Daniel had been...more than cordial. He was friendly and still said good morning. In fact, several mornings a week they shared a cup of coffee before he started working on the renovation if he didn't have to stop by other jobsites first, but there was something ever so slightly removed, something too polite in the way he interacted with her.

He hadn't kissed her since their night together— she'd noticed that, but she hadn't let herself dwell on it because she couldn't blame him. She'd written it off to him being nice and giving her room.

But suddenly it felt like a whole lot of room.

He'd been going to the hospital alone every day, which she thought was natural since Aidan was awake and was doing so much better. She'd wanted to give them time to talk—or not talk—time to interact however brothers interacted. When Aidan had been in the coma, she'd gone to the hospital to support Daniel, but she figured that if she tagged along now, she'd be a third wheel.

They hadn't been out together—for lunch or dinner or a walk …only the coffee at the Sentient Bean. She'd chalked that up to his new schedule that was dictated by Chloe's camp. And now she had learned through her sister, of all people, that Aidan might be having memory issues. Daniel hadn't said a word and that was weird. She had no idea if Aidan's memory loss was confined to Kate—if he remembered Daniel. Or Chloe. Please, God, let him remember his own daughter. It would be devastating for a five-year-old if her father didn't remember her. She wouldn't understand.

But she didn't know, because Daniel hadn't told her.

"Hey, listen, I have to run. My first appointment is going to be at the salon in a half hour. I need to scoot."

After Kate breezed out, Elle stood alone in the sunroom, looking around. Her fingers toyed with the necklace Daniel had given her. She'd set up her easel in the corner and put her brushes in the antique box. She had been working on a painting. It still needed a lot of work, but she was happy with the way it was taking shape.

It suddenly dawned on her that she could stand at her easel right now and paint all day long if she wanted to. When Roger left, she had been forced to regroup and rethink her path. Straight out of art school, her plan had been to be a full-time artist after they got married. Roger had been a business major at the University of Georgia and had graduated a semester ahead of her because she had opted to stick around Savannah and pick up an additional class taught by one of her favorite contemporary artists who had agreed to teach at SCAD for that semester only. Roger had landed a good job with an accounting firm straight out of school and the plan had been for him to work while she finished the extra semester and they would get married after she graduated.

When he'd walked out on her, he'd taken with him her chance to paint full-time. She had to get a job that allowed her to support herself. Teaching hadn't been her first choice, but it was logical and it paid the bills. So, she'd picked up her teaching certificate and had put down her personal art.

As she looked at her painting in progress—a large study of the Christmas garden outside—it hit her. She wasn't so eager to get back to her so-called life in Atlanta as much as she was running away from the risk involved in having another shot at all the things that she once thought would make her happy.

Since the county had made sweeping budget cuts, it was a given that she wouldn't get another job teaching art. If she was lucky, in the fall, she might land an ESE—exceptional student education—position as an art therapist. What was more likely was she would be placed in a curriculum specialist position, which would require her to spend several months training, or they might even put her in some kind of coaching position.

While she loved the chance to work with kids, even elementary art wasn't her dream job. It went downhill from there when she thought of the other nooks and crannies where they might stick her. Those jobs wouldn't make her feel happy or fulfilled.

Not like she'd been while surrounded by her family at their beautiful inn.

Not like she'd been when she'd taught the guests art journaling.

Not like she'd felt when she was with Daniel.

What was wrong with her? If she kept running, not only would she keep getting farther away from who she was and what she liked to do, but she'd push farther away from the man she loved.

She wasn't falling in love with Daniel Quindlin. She was way past falling. She was *in love* with him and it scared the bejeebers out of her.

Suddenly the only place she wanted to be was with Daniel. She hoped it wasn't too late. She knew the only way to find out was to put herself out on the line.

Daniel was up on a ladder in the dining room, surveying the severity of the water damage. It was too bad that Wiladean and Zelda had only cosmetically masked the problem, because it looked as if the moisture had caused some wood rot and that meant repairing it was a bigger job that would take longer. He wasn't looking forward to delivering the news.

"Hey, Daniel," Wiladean called from the doorway. "Can you help me with something, honey?"

"Sure, what do you need?"

Now would be as good a time as any to tell Wiladean what they were facing.

"When I was outside tending to the ivy on the wall, I noticed there was something different about one of the balconies. Would you come and have a look?"

The balcony? What could be wrong with the balcony?

He couldn't help himself. His mind flashed back to

that first morning when he'd seen Elle on the balcony off her room.

He blinked hard. He'd promised himself he wasn't going to do that. He still loved her. Always had. Always would. And because he loved her, he needed to let her figure out things. But it was difficult to give her space when she was living in his head. So, he tried not to think of her.

"You okay, hon?" Wiladean asked.

"I'm fine," he said as they stepped off the stone front porch steps into the front yard.

"Oh, good, because I need you to look up there and tell me what you see."

He squinted up in the direction she was pointing. It was at Elle's balcony.

"Wiladean, I'm sorry, I don't see anything wrong. Can you be more specific? What am I looking for?"

"Really? You can't see that? It's glaring. Are you sure you don't have something in your eye?"

"No, I don't." He started to shade his eyes, but Wiladean grabbed his arm.

"Here, come across the street with me. Maybe you'll be able to see it better from the park."

"Maybe I should go upstairs to the balcony and take a look close up?"

But she was already pulling him into the empty street, across the sidewalk and onto the grass. As he started to turn around, he saw Elle sitting on a blanket with a picnic basket at her side and a small tabletop easel with a canvas on her lap.

"There's Elle," he said.

"Well, yeah," Wiladean said, as if he'd pointed out

the Forsyth fountain a few yards behind her. "That's who I've been trying to get you to see all along."

"But you asked me to look at the balcony."

"Did I say balcony? I meant for you to look at the park. Oh, well, go on over there and you kids have a nice picnic."

"A picnic? She didn't invite me on a picnic." She was painting. He didn't want to disturb her. But then she raised a hand in greeting. He did the same.

"Go on, now," Wiladean said. "I think she's making that painting for you."

He felt almost as bad for Wiladean as he did for himself. She had tried so hard to get the two of them together. But it wasn't going to be. Not right now, anyway. Of course, the county was going to call her and offer her something. She was good at everything she did. They'd be crazy to let someone like her get away.

He'd be crazy to let someone like her get away. But it was out of his control. He wasn't going to force her into anything she didn't want. And she'd turned down his proposal—as unconventional as it was. When it came to relationships, she seemed scared to death of going down the traditional path again after Roger had done such a number on her.

When Elle motioned for him to come closer, he went to her.

"Hi," she said. "Thanks for coming out here. Do you have a minute to sit and talk?"

"I always have time for you."

As he sat down, she moved her easel to the side. The canvas was facing away from him and he couldn't see what she was working on, but he was too busy trying to figure out how to say his bit about wanting to give the long-distance romance a try when she opened her basket and took out two red cups.

She handed one to him. "What's this?"

"It's champagne. I know it's midday and you're working, but I have news. And I can't imagine celebrating it with anyone else but you."

His gut twisted, because he knew what she was about to say.

"You know how I said I was going to leave my decision about whether to stay or go up to fate?"

"You got a job." He tried to infuse enthusiasm into his voice, but he wasn't sure if he was successful.

She nodded. "Curiously enough, it's the job I've always wanted, but not the job I thought I'd get."

"Did the county figure out how to fund your job teaching art?"

"Oh, no, see, that's the thing. They didn't. So, I am going to be teaching art. Right here. At the Forsyth Galloway Inn."

He frowned. "I'm not sure I am following you." He was afraid to read too much into what she said. Afraid that his wishful thinking was clouding his logic. Afraid he was jumping the gun again, like he did when he proposed.

"Are you saying you heard from the county and they *didn't* have a position for you?"

"No, I still haven't heard from them. And it's given me a chance to do a lot of thinking. A very smart man once said, 'Life doesn't give you many second chances. When it does, you better take it.' Daniel, I'm staying right here in Savannah."

His heart squeezed and then turned over in his chest. "I'd say that calls for a toast." He held up his cup and she touched hers to his.

"Does that mean that we can start over and take things slowly?" he asked.

She frowned.

He continued, "I think I was so worried that our time was limited and I thought that putting everything on the fast track would somehow make you want to stay—"

"Daniel, do you love me?"

"I do. I always have and I always will."

She leaned in and kissed him, slow and sweet.

"You don't know how happy that makes me, because I love you, too. And I'm going to go way out on a limb now. I painted this for you."

He raised a brow. "Thank you. I'm honored."

"I hope you will be. Because I don't want to take things slowly. I want to keep them on the same trajectory that they were on before I got scared and almost ruined everything. Or at least I hope I didn't ruin everything. Well, here—"

She turned the canvas around. It was a painting of the Forsyth Galloway Inn. When he looked closer, he saw that she had painted a woman standing on the balcony—the balcony she'd been standing on that first day…the one that Wiladean had him staring at when she'd asked him to come outside.

In the painting, the woman on the balcony was holding a sign that said in the finest calligraphy, *Daniel Quindlin, will you marry me?*

His mouth fell open and it took a moment before he could ask, "Are you proposing to me?"

She squeezed her eyes closed and held her breath, as if bracing herself, and then nodded.

"Of course, I will. Marrying you would make me the happiest man in the world."

A squeal escaped her throat as she got to her knees and threw her arms around him, the sheer force of her joy knocking him backward onto the blanket. They kissed for the longest time.

When they came up for air, she said, "Maybe fate was a better friend than we realized, because she's finally brought us together." Then she laughed and waved her hand as if clearing the air. "*Naaah*, on second thought, Gigi worked harder at bringing us together than fate did. If anyone besides us gets credit, she does. Oh! Which reminds me—"

Elle reached down beside the blanket and picked up another canvas. She held it up over her head.

It said, *HE SAID YES!*

A rousing cheer went up from the balcony where it all started.

Epilogue

On Christmas Day, Daniel and Chloe joined the Boudreau-Clark family at the Forsyth Galloway Inn for a lavish Christmas dinner.

The night before, Daniel and Elle had played Santa for Chloe, showering her with dolls and games and puzzles, among other things. They went all out to give the little girl the best Christmas possible. She was sweet and appreciative, but she couldn't hide her disappointment when she didn't get the one thing she most wanted for Christmas: her father to come home from the hospital.

She held it together pretty well for a five-year-old. Daniel had to admit, better than he might have at that age.

As they were getting ready to sit down to the delicious dinner supplied by Charles Weathersby, family friend and owner of the restaurant, Wila, in downtown Savannah, Daniel got a call on his cell phone.

He nodded to Gigi and then whispered to Elle, "It's time."

He excused himself from the table. "I'll be right back."

"Where are you going, Uncle Daniel?" Chloe asked.

"I just got word that Santa has delivered one more gift for you. Would you like another present or do you think you already have too many?"

Chloe blinked at him. Her sweet little face turned solemn. "Santa already brought me a lot of nice things. It would be okay if he needs to give it to someone who didn't get as much as I got. All I wanted was my daddy, but he's still hurt in the hospital."

She hugged Princess Sweetie Pie close, and for a moment, Daniel was afraid that she might start crying.

"Oh, I don't know, Chloe," he said. "It's very sweet of you to think of others, but you might want to take a look at this before you give it away."

The girl held onto her cat, but didn't respond.

A moment later, Daniel and Kate returned to the dining room, pushing Aidan in a wheelchair.

"Daddy!" Chloe exclaimed. "Santa brought me my daddy for Christmas."

She jumped off her chair and ran over to Aidan, hugging his thigh.

There wasn't a dry eye in the room.

On Christmas Eve, Aidan had been released from the hospital to a rehabilitation center. His doctor had agreed that Aidan was improving enough that he could have a short leave to enjoy Christmas dinner with his daughter, Daniel and the Boudreau-Clark family. He was in good spirits and with Kate's help, he was able to eat most of the offerings on the table. He held his little girl's hand through the entire meal.

After the table was cleared, and everyone was debating how long it would be before they had room for dessert, Daniel pulled Elle out onto the veranda where they could be alone.

"Santa has one last gift and it's for you," he said.

"Daniel, what is this? We've already exchanged gifts."

"This one is special." He smiled at her as he gathered his words. "I know I already proposed—rather badly, actually. And then you proposed, in great style. But there's still something missing."

He pulled out a small blue box from his jacket pocket.

"I feared that it might not be officially official until I put a ring on it."

He opened the box and Elle gasped.

"If you'll let me have a do-over, I'd like to do this right."

Daniel dropped down on one knee and took her hand in his.

"Elle Clark, from the moment I saw you in that library I knew we were destined to be together. Will you make me the happiest man on earth and be my wife?"

"Yes! I can't think of anything that would make me happier. The ring is beautiful."

He slid the traditional two-carat round solitaire onto her delicate finger. Then they sealed the proposal with a kiss to end all kisses.

When they went back into the dining room, the family congratulated them with a champagne toast.

"To the happy couple," the family said in unison.

"This is the best Christmas ever," said Chloe. "Not only did I get my daddy back for Christmas, I got an aunt. Aunt Elle."

* * * * *

Don't miss the next book in the
Savannah Sisters miniseries,
coming in April 2020
from Harlequin Special Edition!

COMING NEXT MONTH FROM

H HARLEQUIN®

SPECIAL EDITION

Available November 19, 2019

#2731 THE RIGHT REASON TO MARRY
The Bravos of Valentine Bay • by Christine Rimmer
Unexpected fatherhood changes everything for charming bachelor Liam Bravo. He wants to marry Karin Killigan, the mother of his child. But Karin won't settle for less than true lasting love.

#2732 MAVERICK CHRISTMAS SURPRISE
Montana Mavericks: Six Brides for Six Brothers • by Brenda Harlen
Rancher Wilder Crawford is in no hurry to get married and start a family—until a four-month-old baby is left on his doorstep on Christmas day!

#2733 THE RANCHER'S BEST GIFT
Men of the West • by Stella Bagwell
Rancher Matthew Waggoner was planning to be in and out of Red Bluff as quickly as possible. But staying with his boss's sister, Camille Hollister, proves to be more enticing than he thought. Will these two opposites be able to work through their differences and get the best Christmas gift?

#2734 IT STARTED AT CHRISTMAS...
Gallant Lake Stories • by Jo McNally
Despite lying on her résumé, Amanda Lowery still manages to land a job designing Halcyon House for Blake Randall—and a place to stay over Christmas. Neither of them have had much to celebrate, but with Blake's grieving nephew staying at Halcyon, they're all hoping for some Christmas magic.

#2735 A TALE OF TWO CHRISTMAS LETTERS
Texas Legends: The McCabes • by Cathy Gillen Thacker
Rehab nurse Bess Monroe is mortified that she accidentally sent out two Christmas letters—one telling the world about her lonely life intead of the positive spin she wanted! And when Jack McCabe, widowed surgeon and father of three, sees the second one, he offers his friendship to get through the holidays. But their pact soon turns into something more...

#2736 THE SOLDIER'S SECRET SON
The Culhanes of Cedar River • by Helen Lacey
When Jake Culhane comes home to Cedar River, he doesn't expect to reconnect with the woman he never forgot. Abby Perkins is still in love with the boy who broke her heart when he enlisted. This could be their first Christmas as a real family—if Abby can find the courage to tell Jake the truth.

YOU CAN FIND MORE INFORMATION ON UPCOMING HARLEQUIN® TITLES, FREE EXCERPTS AND MORE AT WWW.HARLEQUIN.COM.

HSECNM1119

SPECIAL EXCERPT FROM

H HARLEQUIN®

SPECIAL EDITION

*Despite lying on her résumé, Amanda Lowery still
manages to land a job designing Halcyon House for
Blake Randall—and a place to stay over Christmas.
Neither of them have had much to celebrate, but with
Blake's grieving nephew staying at Halcyon, too, they're
all hoping for some Christmas magic.*

Read on for a sneak preview of Jo McNally's
It Started at Christmas…,
a prequel in the Gallant Lake Stories miniseries.

"Amanda, I didn't mean to upset you. I don't ever want to
do anything that scares you."

She sucked in a deep, ragged breath, looking so
terribly lost and sad. Her eyelids fluttered open. She
stared straight ahead, talking to his chest.

"You don't understand, Blake. There are days when…
when everything scares me." Her voice was barely above
a whisper. His heart jumped. He thought of that first day,
when she ended up unconscious in his arms.

Everything scares me.

She'd kicked her shoes off earlier, and in her bare
feet the top of her head barely reached his shoulders. He
put his fingers under her chin and gently tipped her head
back.

He wanted to kiss this woman.

Wait. What?

No. That would be wild. He couldn't kiss her. Shouldn't. But how could he not?

Her hair tumbled off her shoulders and down her back in golden curls. Before he knew it, his free hand was slowly twisting into those curls. She didn't pull away. Didn't look away. He lowered his head until his face was just above hers. He felt her breath on his skin. She smelled like citrus and spice and blueberries and red wine. Her lips parted and she stared at him with her enormous eyes.

"I swear I don't want to scare you, Amanda. But… may I kiss you?" His voice was a raw whisper. "Please let me kiss you."

His words came out as a plea. He'd never begged for anything before in his life. But here he was, begging this sweet woman for a kiss. Ready to drop to his knees if that was what it took. He heard his father's voice in his head, mocking his weakness. That was when he started to straighten, started to come to his senses. Then he heard her whispered answer.

"Yes."

Was there any sweeter word in the world? Adrenaline surged through his body, and his hand tightened in her hair. His eyes opened to meet those two oceans of blue. Dangerous blue. Deep enough to drown in.

She was frightened, but she was trusting him. And that realization scared him to death.

Don't miss It Started at Christmas… *by Jo McNally, available December 2019 wherever Harlequin® Special Edition books and ebooks are sold.*

Harlequin.com

Looking for more satisfying love stories
with community and family at their core?

Check out **Harlequin® Special Edition**
and **Love Inspired®** books!

New books available every month!

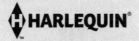

Looking for inspiration in tales
of hope, faith and heartfelt romance?

Check out **Love Inspired**® and
Love Inspired® **Suspense** books!

New books available every month!

CONNECT WITH US AT:

Facebook.com/groups/HarlequinConnection

Facebook.com/HarlequinBooks

Twitter.com/HarlequinBooks

Instagram.com/HarlequinBooks

Pinterest.com/HarlequinBooks

ReaderService.com

Love Harlequin romance?

DISCOVER.

Be the first to find out about promotions, news and exclusive content!

Facebook.com/HarlequinBooks

Twitter.com/HarlequinBooks

Instagram.com/HarlequinBooks

Pinterest.com/HarlequinBooks

ReaderService.com

EXPLORE.

Sign up for the Harlequin e-newsletter and download a free book from any series at **TryHarlequin.com.**

CONNECT.

Join our Harlequin community to share your thoughts and connect with other romance readers!
Facebook.com/groups/HarlequinConnection

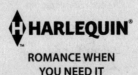

HARLEQUIN®

**ROMANCE WHEN
YOU NEED IT**